Supper Club Chronicles

Supper Club Chronicles is hosted by your author, Susan Higgins-Krais. To join other fans of the Supper Club Chronicles, go to www.SusanHigginsKrais.com.

- Check out recipes from the book!
- Share your own Supper Club stories!
- Enjoy an online chat with Susan or other Supper Clubbers!

There's plenty of room at the table, and we've got a seat just for you…

Website: www.SusanHigginsKrais.com

Facebook: Susan Higgins-Krais/Author

Instagram: susan_higginskrais@Instagram

Twitter: @KraisSusan

Email: susanhigginskrais@gmail.com

It's About Time

The Supper Club Chronicles

(Book 1)

Susan Higgins-Krais

It's About Time by Susan Higgins-Krais

ISBN: 978-1-7356179-0-9

Original Cover Design by Juliana Gyimesi

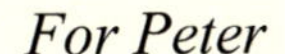

For Peter

It's About Time

The Supper Club Chronicles

(Book 1)

Prologue

The bony fourteen-year-old, her coal-black hair cascading over her pillow, awoke to the smell of turkey roasting in the oven. She slipped into her ill-fitting jeans and favorite knit sweater—the one with six rows of hearts, each another color of the rainbow, running horizontally across the top. Then she brushed her tangled locks smooth and nimbly wove them into a French braid. After fastening the two Velcro straps on each of her sneakers, she bounded down the stairs, turned on the TV, and adjusted the rabbit ears.

Lying on the gold and brown shag carpet, whose colors camouflaged a multitude of stains, she rested her chin in her hands. She loved watching the Macy's Thanksgiving Day Parade and dreamed of living in New York City someday, perhaps disappearing into the bustle of the Big Apple.

At noon, she went to help her mother prepare side dishes, while her father planted himself in front of the television to watch football. The kitchen window over the chipped porcelain sink was open, but the savory scent of turkey stuffed with bread, eggs, sausage, and spinach cloaked the room.

"How was the parade?" asked her mother as she plucked a cigarette from a soft aqua pack.

"Awesome. Cool floats this year."

"Grab me some matches from the living room, would you? And bring this beer to your father." The mother opened the fridge, pried a can of Budweiser from the plastic ring that secured it to the remaining three cans, and handed it to her daughter.

Careful not to make any noise, the girl crept into the living room, picked up the two crushed cans from the coffee table, and placed the beer on the tarnished silver coaster resting next to her father's shin. Then she snatched a pack of matches from the basket on the end table.

"Here you go, Mom," she said as she returned to the kitchen, striking the match to the flint and holding it out. Her mother leaned forward and sucked deeply on the filters, the purplish bruise on her left cheekbone barely visible. "What can I help you with?" the girl asked.

"Why don't you peel those potatoes?" the mother said, gesturing to the bag of Yukon Golds beside the toaster.

The girl grabbed the garbage can and placed it next to the kitchen table, where a bowl awaited her. "Oh my gosh, Mom, you won't believe what happened in school yesterday." She fished around the utensil drawer and retrieved a potato peeler. With the bag of potatoes, she settled into a chair and got to work. "Peter Jones has a crush on Julie Mount, and he wanted her to pay attention to him, so he came to school with no eyebrows!" Using the peeler to imitate a razor, she mimed the act of shaving off an eyebrow. "Can you believe it? He looked like an alien." She scraped the peeler along the spud, the skin falling into the bin. "The teacher made him go to the office, and we didn't see him for the rest of the day."

"That boy sounds like he has a few screws loose."

"Smells good in here," said the girl's father, entering the kitchen and emitting a sound like a croaking bullfrog. He reached into the refrigerator and pulled out two more beers before heading back to the living room.

When the girl finished peeling, her mother took the bowl of potatoes and dropped them into a pot of boiling water. "Why don't you make the casserole?" the mother said. "The beans are in the freezer and the soup and onions are in the pantry."

The Thanksgiving menu never changed. The girl looked forward every year to turkey, filling, green bean casserole, sweet potatoes, mashed potatoes, and canned cranberry sauce. After pulling the green beans from the freezer, she ran them under hot water to defrost them before dumping them into a baking dish. Next, she opened the pantry door and scanned the wire rack shelves for the cream of mushroom soup and dried onions. At the sight of the yardstick resting against the bottom shelf, she cringed, a sick feeling churning in her stomach.

"You know," her mother said, "it won't be long before you can get a summer job in a restaurant kitchen. Money doesn't grow on trees."

"Hey," her father yelled from his perch on the sofa, "can one of you bring me a Jack and Coke on ice?"

"He wasn't always like this," said her mother under her breath as she handed the bottle of Jack Daniels to her daughter.

By late afternoon, the turkey and fixings were ready, and she couldn't wait to eat.

"I'll set the table, Mom." It was the one day all year that they ate off of her mother's good china, which had once belonged to the girl's grandmother. Each ivory plate and serving dish was adorned with tiny blue roses, and when they used the china, they drank from delicate goblets that her mother had received as a wedding present. She felt like royalty when she got to eat a meal with such fancy place settings.

"Just be careful," warned her mother. "You know how much they mean to me."

"Don't worry, Mom," she said as she stacked the plates and serving dishes, balancing three goblets on top. As she stepped forward, she didn't notice the small puddle of water left behind from ice her father had dropped when he refilled his drink. The slick sole of her treadless Reeboks offered little assistance as she lost her balance, but she quickly planted her foot, snagged the goblets, and saved them from crashing to the tile floor.

Aware of her heart pounding in her chest, she swallowed the anxious feeling growing in her belly. *Stay calm*, she told herself. *No one noticed.* She gingerly placed the china on the table, her hands shaking just enough to cause the goblet she set down next to her father's plate to teeter. She heard herself gasp and, as if watching a movie in slow motion, reached for the glass to steady it, but it toppled over, leaving a spray of fine crystal shards on the place setting.

"Oh no!" cried her mother before covering her mouth with her hands.

At the sound of her father's voice, the girl's head jolted toward the living room.

"What was that?" he roared as he got up and steadied himself before stumbling toward the kitchen.

The girl stood frozen, her eyes darting from her mother to the kitchen doorway. "I'm so sorry, Mom. I didn't mean it." She pivoted and dashed out the back door, her father in pursuit, his voice echoing in her ears as he slapped the yardstick against the chipped cedar shakes again and again and again.

CHAPTER 1

"There are two days in my calendar: this day and that day."

— Martin Luther

Beep-beep-beep… Maura's alarm jolted her out of much-needed deep sleep. Last night was the first time she had not woken up from the recurring nightmare of Paul's lifeless body beside the coffee table, his face lying in an expansive pool of blood. She breathed in deeply, then slowly exhaled and opened her eyes. The morning sun shone through the blinds, the slats casting a shadow of muted stripes on the cream-colored blanket. She propped her pillow against the cherry wood headboard of the old four-poster bed. Then she sat up and inhaled deeply again, until her breath caught in her chest. She was fully awake now.

Two weeks had passed, but Maura still had a hard time accepting the reality of Paul's death. She felt as though she'd been sucked out of a plane window, her body free-falling toward the cold hard ground below. Paul had been her safety net and now he was gone.

She fixed her gaze on the bedroom door. Ordinarily, Paul would have appeared in the next minute or two, holding a cup of coffee for each of them. As Maura would have leaned against the headboard, Paul would have sat on the edge of the bed to discuss their plans for the day. Then he'd head off to work, and she would drive to her gym, The Coastal Club. However, today was no ordinary day; she wouldn't be going anywhere.

Snippets of the funeral repast flashed through her brain: greeting friends, hugging relatives, thanking them for their condolences. During the meal, she'd sat between her son, Dean, and her daughter, Stephanie, but had only managed to push the penne vodka and chicken piccata from one side of her plate to the other. *Keep nodding your head and smiling*, she'd thought as she stood, resting her hands on the shoulders of her grandson while he joked with his cousins.

Maura pushed aside the covers and sat on the edge of the bed for a moment before planting her feet on the soft honeycomb-patterned ikat rug below, preparing to face another day that she wasn't prepared for.

* * * * * * * * * * * * *

As Maura entered the bedroom again, minute specks of dust floated through the shaft of afternoon sunlight that sliced through the slanted blinds. Struggling to find some kind of closure, she decided to go through Paul's belongings. She opened the closet door to reveal a long, narrow walk-in with barely enough room for two wardrobes. They had talked about remodeling it for years but had never gotten around to it. Now it wouldn't be necessary. She removed her husband's clothes and sorted them into two piles—one for Dean and one for rummage.

How strange. She'd been talking to herself all day but hadn't uttered a word. She hadn't turned on the television or put on any music, yet there hadn't been a single moment of silence in her mind. As she'd puttered, her thoughts had raced from one memory to another. It was as if the contents of the house, which until now had remained part of a backdrop, had come into focus, each triggering another snapshot through the lens of the past.

Sorting through the tie rack, Maura remembered how it was once laden with ties, the colors, patterns, and widths changing with the styles of the day. Now, there were half as many; times had changed, and the dress codes had grown more relaxed. She gathered the remaining ties and tossed them on the rummage pile, but when a swatch of yellow caught her eye, she had to blink several times to hold back tears. The tie had been a present from Dean to his father.

Father's Day marked one of many occasions when the family had gathered. She smiled as she remembered celebrating last Father's Day with her husband, her children and their spouses, and the grandchildren. Gathered around the dining room table, they had talked and laughed as Maura doled out plates of trifle for dessert. Her eight-year-old granddaughter, Sally, requested that same trifle every year on her birthday. After dinner, Dean had presented Paul with the yellow necktie. Although Dean had worried it was a bit cliché to gift a tie on Father's Day, that slim piece of silk had immediately topped the ranks as Paul's new favorite.

With Paul's side of the closet emptied, she moved on to the chest of drawers. Once again, tears pooled in her eyes when she spotted a sweatshirt—a birthday gift from Stephanie long ago. The front showed a picture of Jake and Sally that Maura recalled fondly. She and Stephanie had been walking through the mall one day with Stephanie's two children. Stephanie had been pushing Sally in an umbrella stroller, while Maura had walked alongside, clasping Jake's little hand in hers. Stephanie had spotted the pop-up kiosk, and the photographer had captured a moment of pure bliss on the grandkids' faces, which he embossed on the front of the sweatshirt. Paul had worn it so often that the blue of Sally's eyes had faded to gray.

When she finished sorting Paul's clothes, she set each pile on the floor and headed to the kitchen. Last week, her kitchen was filled with family and friends, and her refrigerator was filled with casseroles. This week, she'd declined offers of both company and food, yearning for a small sense of normalcy, at least at dinnertime. Maura and Paul had enjoyed cooking together. They used to joke about the endless television channels to choose from, but unless they were watching sports, the cooking channels usually hogged the screen. This week, cooking had not been a problem for Maura, but eating had been. After a few uninspired mouthfuls of baked ziti, she wrapped the rest and opened the freezer, which was stuffed with a smorgasbord of her own home-cooked entrees. Tonight's creation became yet another layer in the growing tower of aluminum foil bricks.

The sun had barely set when Maura slipped into her pajamas, crawled into bed, and picked up the remote from the nightstand. She turned on the Food Network and settled in for the night. The stream of programs offered a brief respite from the cyclone of emotions swirling around her head. Eventually, her eyes felt heavy. She turned off the TV and escaped into a fitful sleep.

* * * * * * * * * * * * *

At 5:30 a.m., the alarm flashed and blared out its all-too-familiar beeps. A melancholy mood, which caught Maura off-guard each morning, had wrapped its arms around her once again. She closed her eyes, counted backward from five to one, and willed herself out of the bed and down the stairs.

After gulping down her morning joe, Maura returned to her bedroom and grabbed a sweatshirt and her belongings. With her favorite pale-pink hoodie over her pj's and a gym bag over her shoulder, she acknowledged a feeling of normalcy. Then she returned to the kitchen and exited to the garage. Maura's SUV looked shabby next to Paul's two-seater Corvette. She sighed as she recalled how he'd spent hours puttering with the engine or buffing the exterior. Cruising in the classic, candy-apple-red sports car had been one of his favorite pastimes, and nothing had made him happier than showing "her" off at the annual classic car show. Maura used to jokingly refer to the car as "the other woman."

A wave of grief washed over her as she shifted her SUV into reverse.

Navigating the route to the gym on autopilot, she thought about the four women she had been changing next to in the locker room for years. Kara, her closest friend, was an elementary school teacher. Prior to Maura resigning to stay home with the children, she and Kara had taught together. They'd remained close and eventually both joined The Coastal

Club.

Maura didn't socialize with the remaining three women, at least not outside the health club. They'd never exchanged cell phone numbers or friended each other on Facebook, but they had engaged in an ongoing locker room conversation about their families, jobs, and relationships for nearly two decades. Josie, the oldest, was a licensed family counselor with a calm, sensible demeanor. Nicole, the youngest, was a real estate agent with a vivacious personality forever in search of Mister Right, and Lonnie, a high-powered lawyer, battled weight issues as often as she battled court cases. The five were an unconventional group with an unconventional friendship. Work or workouts were not what brought them together. Instead, an intangible quality of connectedness and concern served as the foundation for their lasting relationship, and Maura knew that she could rely on each of them for support and advice.

"Good morning!" chirped the girl at the front desk as Maura entered.

Maura swiped her tag and smiled before making her way to the locker room. She longed for an escape from reality, and the gym had always been a place to do that. Sometimes she craved a hard workout that left her feeling exhausted and exhilarated. Other times she sought a class that challenged her both physically and mentally. Today she would use her swim as a vehicle to meditate.

She slid into the pool and lost herself in the rhythm of her stroke. Time became suspended. She thought of nothing but the feel of the water and the stretch of her muscles as she glided up and down the lane. An hour later, she placed her hands on the pool deck and hoisted herself out of the water.

After tossing her goggles into her swim bag, she wrapped herself in a towel and headed for the locker room. The swim had relaxed her body and cleared her mind. She was ready to face the day and her friends.

As Maura neared her locker, she saw Lonnie approaching with a giddy grin on her face. A few days earlier, Lonnie, a self-described control freak who couldn't control her food intake, had returned from her annual two-week stay at an all-inclusive resort that specialized in intensive weight loss.

"Well, what do you think?" Lonnie said. "Have I been transformed? Do I look as good as I feel?"

"Lonnie, you look fabulous. Now you just have to stick with it."

"That's my problem. I have no willpower. Look at you, Maura, how do you do it?"

"I work out—a lot." Maura chuckled. "Maybe you'll meet me for a run sometime?"

"Oh, Lord no. I'll stick with thirty minutes on the elliptical. I use that time to check email. And as far as running goes, girl, once my feet hit the ground, I start running and don't stop until I turn off my office light and head for home."

Maura clasped Lonnie's hands in hers and squeezed them lightly. "Sit down, Lonnie. I have to tell you some terrible news." Her shoulders rose toward her ears and then fell back into place.

Lonnie sat, eyes locked on her friend, and listened to Maura describe the events surrounding Paul's death.

Two weeks earlier, Maura's husband, Paul, had sat down to watch the Phillies' opening-day game. Paul loved baseball and had been looking forward to that game all winter. He'd already settled onto the sofa and taken a gulp of his ice-cold beer. Maura had settled in next to him, sipping her own beer and smiling nonstop. She loved opening day as much as Paul did, and watching it together was a ritual they'd enjoyed from the start of their relationship. While in grad school, they would hunker down in Paul's tiny apartment, drinking and munching as Paul commented on each play. Once they'd graduated and gotten jobs, they even took the day off to watch the game. And when the children were young, they'd go so far as to let them stay home from school for the big day.

"Hey, would you like me to make some nachos?" Maura offered.

Paul's eyes widened. "Sure!"

She went into the kitchen, tuned thc counter television to the game, and pulled out the makings for nachos. She browned some ground turkey and onion, spread the mixture on a cookie sheet, topped it with taco chips, added the rest of the fixings, and popped it into the oven. After setting the timer, she remembered a load of wash that needed to go in the dryer, so she headed to the basement. But while lifting the lid of the washing machine, she heard a loud thud.

"Paul!" she called out. "What was that? Are you okay?"

No answer.

She sprinted to the family room and gasped. "Paul!"

Paul lay facedown across the collapsed coffee table. Blood had pooled on the beige Berber carpet, flowing from the broken nose he'd sustained when his face slammed against the surface of the wooden tabletop.

Maura lowered him gently to the carpet and flipped him onto his back before bolting to the kitchen. She ripped her cell phone from its charger and was startled by the jarring beep of the oven timer. She slammed it off. It was difficult to steady the phone as her thumb swiped and her fingers punched in an effort to dial 911. Then, feeling faint, she placed the phone on the counter and pressed the speaker before grabbing on for support. She inhaled and exhaled deeply until she heard a voice on the line. "It's my husband!" she shouted. "He's fainted. I don't know what's wrong. Please hurry!"

Maura paced and prayed, telling herself she could will Paul back to life. She watched as the EMTs hovered over his body. Then she leaned over him on the ambulance ride, pleading with him to hang on. Later, at the hospital, when the doctor explained that there was nothing he could do, she wanted to slap his face and call him a liar. Instead, she collapsed into the nearest chair, sobbing into her hands as she allowed his words to sink in. If her children had not been by her side consoling her, she might have convinced herself that she and the kids were merely waiting for Paul to emerge from the operating room after taking care of that trick knee. Despite blaming it for consistent bogies while golfing, he'd always refused to do anything about it.

Lonnie released her hands from Maura's grasp and swiped her glistening cheeks. "Oh, Maura, I'm so sorry. I didn't know."

"I know you didn't," said Maura as she leaned forward and embraced her friend.

"I should be consoling you," Lonnie whimpered.

"Don't you worry. There will be time for that. Right now, I think I'm still in shock."

Maura glanced toward the lockers and saw Josie approaching. Josie was easy to spot, not only due to her height and blue-striped pixie haircut but also due to her love of neon-colored workout wear.

Josie wrapped her arm around Maura's shoulder and squeezed gently. "I hope you didn't mind my asking Kara for your cell number, but along with my condolences, I wanted to send that list of counselors and support groups. Did I overstep?"

Maura smiled. "Of course not. I appreciate it, but to be honest I haven't even looked at the list yet."

"I'm not surprised," said Josie, pulling a tissue from her hot-pink polka-dot gym shorts and handing it to Lonnie.

"Maura," Lonnie said, "you know if there's any legal issue you want to discuss, you can reach out to me."

"I appreciate it, and I'll keep that in mind. Right now, all I need is a hot shower." Maura removed the shampoo and conditioner from her gym bag and made her way to the shower area. She pulled the curtain closed, turned on the water, and let the warmth envelop her, unsure whether the water trickling down her cheeks was a stream of tears or simply spray from the showerhead.

Exiting the stall wrapped in one of the club's utilitarian white towels, she strode to the vanity area, the usual bounce in her step missing.

"I'm so happy to see you back here," said Kara, who was straightening her hair.

Maura dragged over a stool from an adjacent station and sat down next to her closest friend. "It felt great to get back into the pool." Her eyes went glassy. "I get so overwhelmed sometimes. I never realized how much I depended on Paul."

"I hope the kids are at least a comfort."

"Of course. Dean is coming over this afternoon to help me deal with some paperwork. I don't know how I'd get through this without him and Stephanie."

Kara turned off the straightener and leaned over to hug Maura tightly. "I know I keep repeating myself, but please let me know if you need anything."

"Thanks. You're a good friend."

Maura returned the hug, then headed to her locker. She slid out her gym bag and fished around for her clothes.

"Oh no!" she exclaimed, pulling out a pair of sweatpants twice as long as she. "I picked up Paul's sweatpants by mistake." She shook her head as she shoved the pants back into her gym bag and reached for her drawstring bottoms.

"No worries," Nicole called from the next bay of lockers. "Borrow mine if you don't mind the Nicole's Realty logo on the hip. I only wore them over my spin shorts on the way in." She appeared in Maura's bay and paused before handing over the pants. "By the way, I didn't get a chance to speak to you after the funeral. I want you to know that my heart breaks for you and your family." Then she wrapped an arm around Maura's waist and, with a sympathetic frown, cried, "Come on, girls, group hug!"

Nicole, Josie, Kara, and Lonnie locked arms around Maura, and for the first time since assembling a nacho platter in her kitchen, Maura felt like she was standing on solid ground.

CHAPTER 2

"Memories are timeless treasures
of the heart."

– Unknown

Maura's heartbeat quickened at the sound of the front door opening.

"Mom?"

"Oh, Dean," she called from her bedroom. "It's you."

"The one and only."

"I'll be right down," she said, scolding herself for being so jumpy.

Maura walked downstairs and joined her son in the foyer. She cradled his face in her hands and looked into his army-green eyes. With his short scruffy beard and faded Phish T-shirt, he looked more like a carefree millennial than a responsible husband and father. "How are you doing?"

Dean sighed. "To be honest, I still can't wrap my head around it. I keep waiting for Dad to call or text. A few times,

I've picked up my cell and pressed his name in my contacts or started to text, and then it all comes rushing back." His eyes filled, and Maura held him close.

After a moment, she gestured toward the family room. "Let's sit."

As they sank into the plush, tufted, oversized sofa, she caught her reflection in the flat-screen television between the bookcases and realized how gaunt her face had become. But this wasn't the time for self-deprecation.

"I'd like to share some information with you," she said. "My friend Josie from the health club is a family counselor. She gave me a list of therapists and bereavement groups in the area. I know you aren't a fan of sharing your feelings, and neither am I." She shrugged her shoulders and took a deep breath. "But dealing with Dad's sudden death will take time, and you may need a professional to help you navigate through this. I may contact someone myself." She patted his knee.

Dean squeezed her hands and smiled faintly. "Thanks, Mom. I'll have to think about it."

After a moment of silence, Maura brought up a new topic. "I appreciate your help. I'm a little overwhelmed."

"No worries. I may have to take a call or two, but other than that, I'm all yours. Now, what do you want to tackle first?"

"To be honest, I'm not sure where to start. Your dad always handled the finances, and now I have to deal with bank accounts, insurance, the deed to the house, credit card accounts—"

"Slow down, Mom. Grab your laptop. Let me see what we're dealing with."

An hour later, they were still ticking items off her to-do list and making a list of places they needed to go.

* * * * * * * * * * * * * *

After a long day of errands, Maura pulled the SUV into the garage while Dean tapped away on his phone screen. She glanced at Paul's car, and her breath caught in her chest. "I don't know what to do with Dad's Corvette."

Dean looked at the car and smiled. "He did love that thing, but I don't have any interest in keeping it, and I don't think Stephanie does either." He tapped his fingers against his lips. "Maybe Kyle knows someone at the dealership who could take it off your hands."

With so many things to think about and decide upon, Maura felt like a conjoined twin who had been separated from her other half. Over the years, she and Paul had mastered how to work in tandem, each functioning separately but combining their efforts to create a whole. "Sure, that sounds good," she said.

Entering the kitchen behind Dean, she set her bag on the large distressed farm table just as her cell announced a call from Stephanie.

"Hi, Steph," she said into the phone. "Dean and I just walked in. Let me put you on speaker."

"Hi, Dean," Steph said.

"What up, Sis?"

"Listen, I'm going to pick up some pizzas. Kyle, the kids, and I are coming over to Mom and Dad's"—she stopped short, seeming to reset her brain before continuing—"at seven for dinner. How does that sound, Mom?" Without waiting for a response, she added, "I hope you can all come too, Dean."

Not waiting for an answer was typical of Stephanie, a raven-haired firecracker who loved impromptu outings, festive dinners, and pool parties—a trait she shared with her father. When Stephanie was growing up, the two of them would conspire to make every outing an adventure, assigning every celebration a theme.

"I'll check with the boss and text you," Dean said. "I think it'll be cool, though."

"Great. See you at seven. Love you, Mom."

* * * * * * * * * * * * *

By seven thirty, everyone was gathered around the table in Maura's spacious kitchen. Drinks were poured and plates were filled. But before the first steaming slice of pepperoni pizza could be devoured, Dean's fourteen-year-old son, Sam, tapped his glass with his fork. "Attention, everyone!" he bellowed. "Can I have your attention!" He commanded rather than asked. "As we all know, at any special family dinner, Pop would always read a poem before we ate. This being the first dinner here without him"—Sam swallowed—"I would like to share a poem:

"To be an Italian means many things
We eat pasta, we drink wine, we dance and we sing
The head of the house is a man tough as nails
But sweeter than honey and full of wise tales
An Italian grandfather is his grandkid's best friend
Always quick with a joke and a swift hand to lend
Even though his time's passed,
He still looks down from above

Benedici questa casa con gioia e amore
Bless this house with joy and love."

The first to gather herself, Stephanie addressed the family. "I think this is a perfect time to share something I've brought along for Mom, Dean, and myself."

She left the table and returned with an oversized light-brown leather satchel. Reaching in, she pulled out three DNA kits and handed one each to her mother and brother, keeping the last one for herself. "Mom, I was thinking about the time you, Dad, and I saw that commercial for DNA kits. You weren't that interested, but Dad was intrigued. It got me thinking that tracing our DNA would be a way for all of us to learn more about you. And just as importantly, I can't think of a better way to honor Dad's legacy than to research his family. I know he'd be pleased if we did this, and I think you'll find it interesting too. Who knows? Maybe we have some distant relatives we've never met."

A jolt like an electric current surged through Maura's body. Her mind raced as quickly as her pulse, but she stayed quiet.

"Awesome idea!" Dean said. "What do you think, Mom? We don't know much about your extended family, and this feels like a great way to stay connected to Dad. The more we find out about his roots, the less final his death will seem." Dean blinked back the water filling his eyes and read from the box. "It says you can even build a family tree based on the results." He turned to Stephanie. "Great idea, Sis."

Maura masked her anxiety with a forced smile and robotic nodding. She had done it at the funeral, and she could do it again now.

"How does it work?" asked Jake, Stephanie's son.

"I want to take the test!" squealed Sally. "I always get smiley face stickers on my tests. What's a BMA test anyway?"

"It's D-N-A!" shouted her ten-year-old brother.

Stephanie whipped her head and fixed her gaze on Jake, who lowered his eyes and mumbled an apology to his sister. "Even though we know we're Irish and Italian," said Stephanie, "maybe we can identify the specific regions we're from."

"Yeah, then we can plan a family trip to visit each place," said Sam, grabbing his father's kit. "Let's see how to do this." He read the directions. "Seems simple enough. You spit into a test tube, seal it, and mail it to the lab in a pre-labeled envelope. Six to eight weeks later, you get the results online."

Maura felt the room closing in around her. She grabbed her glass, hurried to the fridge, and pressed it against the water dispenser. *After all these years, I can't believe I have to deal with this now!* She guzzled some water, filled her glass again, then returned to the table.

"Mom, take your test first thing tomorrow morning," ordered Stephanie. "Dean will do the same. I'll pick them up in the afternoon and mail them out on Monday." She leaned over and gave her mother a hug. "Isn't this exciting?"

"Dad," said Sally, "can I have another slice of pizza?"

Drinks were refilled, pizza boxes were emptied, and eventually, the conversation died down.

"I think we should make Friday night dinner a tradition," said Stephanie as she turned to her mother. "Would you like that?"

"I would love that, honey."

"Great idea, babe," agreed Stephanie's husband, Kyle, as he glanced at his watch. "I hate to be a downer, but it's getting late and Jake has baseball practice early tomorrow morning."

"We should go too," said Maddie, Dean's wife.

"Thank you for the poem, Sam," whispered Maura. "Pop would have been so proud." She pulled Sam close and squeezed him before opening her arms and wrapping them around Jake and Sally too. She planted a kiss on top of each little head. "Whose idea was it to get pizza tonight?"

"It was mine," declared Jake.

"Yeah, but I thought of the pepperoni," added Sally.

"Well, it was delicious. Thank you both."

The adults said their goodbyes and the group clambered down the narrow hallway toward the front door.

"Maddie, I'll be out in a minute," called Dean from the kitchen. He bent down and wrapped his long arms around his mother. "You were very quiet tonight. I think the day has taken a toll on you. Try to get some sleep."

Alone at last, Maura wandered through the house and turned off lights, her thoughts as twisted as a pretzel. Longing for an escape from what had become the second unimaginable scenario in two weeks, she climbed the stairs, crawled into bed, and retreated into a cocoon of covers. But sleep eluded her. Minutes turned into hours as she tossed and turned, dozing for what felt like an instant, only to awaken again and stare at the ceiling. Turning onto her stomach, she buried her face in her pillow. With clenched fists, she pounded the mattress until exhausted, then finally fell asleep as the first light of day cast a pink glow on the light-gray walls.

* * * * * * * * * * * * * *

Maura awoke at 9:00 a.m. filled with overwhelming nervous

energy. Not ready to dwell on the events of last night, she headed to the gym—a place where she could escape reality, at least for a little while. Once there, she made a beeline for the spin studio. Small, dark, and dimly lit, the room had a cave-like ambiance. An LCD projector dangled from the ceiling, shining a patchwork of information onto a screen at the front of the room next to the instructor's bike. Data such as heart rate and total calories burned for each participant were on display for all to see. The only other faint glow came from the individual cell-phone-sized monitors attached to each bike; they recorded pedal speed, power, and distance covered during the virtual ride.

"Okay," said the instructor into his headset as he pressed play on the stereo. "Warm-up's yours!"

Maura didn't know why spin classes took place in semi-darkness; what she did know was that for their sixty-minute duration, nothing else existed. Music pulsed, and pedal speeds changed from heart-racing quick to quad-burning slow. The instructor's passion was contagious, creating palpable energy in the room. At the end of class, everyone was spent. Faces were flushed, bodies were sweaty, and endorphins were firing. An overall euphoric mood seemed to fill the space. Class members, after wiping down their bikes, usually exited the room in clusters. They chatted about the challenging ride and joked about how and when they had failed or succeeded. It was the same conversation after every class, and everyone seemed to love it.

After refilling her water bottle in the lobby, Maura chatted with a few others as she sauntered toward the women's locker room. Nothing was better after a sweat-soaking spin class than a warm soapy shower. Alone in her stall, Maura squeezed a dollop of shampoo onto her palm and massaged her scalp. But like the frothy lather in her hair, last night's concerns bubbled up to the surface once again. She forced them out of her mind by focusing on the advice in an article Josie had emailed. The author had suggested taking care of the things you could control rather than dwelling on those you couldn't. Maura finished up in the shower, dressed quickly, and made her way home to do just that.

* * * * * * * * * * * * * *

Seated at her kitchen table, Maura called Stephanie. "Hi, Steph, I want to ask you—well actually, Kyle—for a favor. Do you think he can take care of selling Dad's car? I don't need it, and rather than having it gather dust, I'd like to pass it on to someone who will enjoy it. Unless you want it?"

"Thanks, Mom, but I'm not interested in it." Her voice cracked. "That car was Dad's baby, but Kyle will be happy to help. Don't worry, he'll handle everything."

"Thank you, honey. Tell him I appreciate it. By the way, how are you managing?"

"I have my moments, but I think I'm okay." Like her father, Stephanie had an uncanny ability to compartmentalize her emotions. Maura wasn't so sure this was always a good thing, but it was probably better than pushing feelings down, stewing about things, or ignoring issues the way she and Dean did.

"I told your brother it might be a good idea to reach out to a counselor or bereavement group. Maybe you should consider it too."

"Sure, send me the list. By the way, have you taken your

DNA test yet?"

The mere mention of the test made Maura feel as if a hive of bees was swarming through her veins. "No, I didn't get to it yet."

"Really? Do it now. Kyle and I will stop over later to collect the kit and the car."

A few moments later, Maura hung up and glared at her new nemesis in the cardboard box.

Shortly after dark, Stephanie and Kyle arrived. "Come on in," said Maura as she met them on the front porch. "Where are the kids?"

"We dropped them off at the Foys' house for a neighborhood movie night," Stephanie explained as she and Kyle followed Maura to the family room. "We're heading back over there after we pick up Dad's car." Stephanie suddenly stopped short and gasped.

Maura understood that the empty space where the coffee table and area rug had once rested had thrown Stephanie off.

"Oh, Mom, this is so surreal!" She moved toward Maura, who embraced her.

"I know," agreed Maura as she rubbed Stephanie's back, which rose and fell with quiet sobs. "Kyle, the keys to Paul's car are on the keyring in the kitchen. Why don't you grab them?" She held Stephanie for a moment more. "Are you okay?" she asked before releasing her grasp.

"I'm fine," Stephanie said as she pressed her fingertips into her damp eyelids. "I didn't see that coming!"

Maura picked up the DNA kit from the end table and handed it to Stephanie.

"We're only weeks away from getting the results," said Stephanie as Kyle returned with the keys. "Okay, we'd better get going." Then she grimaced. "I'm sorry, Mom. That was insensitive. Do you want us to stay? We don't have to go to movie night."

"Oh no," insisted Maura. "You go and have fun. It will be good for the kids to see that life goes on. Last night was wonderful, but I'll be fine on my own tonight."

Maura glanced out the family room window one last time at the Corvette on the driveway, moonlight reflecting off the gloss of its highly polished hood.

"You're doing the right thing, Mom," said Stephanie as she gave Maura one final embrace.

As Maura waved goodbye, she watched the taillights of the Corvette fade into the darkness. Her shoulders shook and her chest heaved as the sound of her sobs overtook the quiet house.

CHAPTER 3

"With endless time, nothing is special. With no loss or sacrifice, we can't appreciate what we have"

– *Mitch Albom, in The Time Keeper*

Monday morning arrived unseasonably cold and rainy, but Maura didn't mind. She was glad the weekend was over so she could slip into the comfort of her weekday routine.

Monday morning workouts meant one thing: a suffer-fest, or as the health club class schedule called it, Small-Group Extreme Boot Camp. Maura, along with eleven other members, would spend an hour doing an ever-changing routine of running, climbing, crawling, lifting, jumping, pushing, and pulling. Similar to spin class, time didn't exist for those sixty minutes, and Maura focused on sweating from every last pore. By the end, she felt exhausted yet energized.

"This time is going to be different," declared Lonnie as she and Nicole entered the locker room.

"Good morning, ladies," Maura called from her locker bay. "Nicole, I have your sweatpants. Thanks again for the loan."

"Anytime," replied Nicole.

Lonnie dropped her bag on the bench and opened a locker near Maura's. "I just told Nicole how positive I feel about losing weight for good this time." She whipped off her sweats to reveal a slightly slimmer figure. "For the next month, I'll FaceTime with my nutrition counselor twice a week. She'll supply healthy recipes, and I'll update her on my daily food diary. She even put me in touch with a personal trainer in our area. I met with her over the weekend and really liked her." Lonnie reached into her gym bag. "See? Here's her business card."

Lonnie handed each of them a bright yellow card emblazoned with red letters. On one side in bold letters, it said *IT'S ABOUT TIME!* along with the trainer's contact info. The other side listed her qualifications and certifications.

"I love the name," Lonnie said. "*It's about time* to get started on a healthier lifestyle. *It's about time* to stop making excuses."

"It's about time you make yourself a priority," added Maura.

The women high-fived before Lonnie continued. "I'll meet with her once a week, and she'll create an exercise plan based on The Coastal Club's class schedule and equipment." She winked at Maura. "I may stray from the elliptical machine yet."

Maura smiled. "It certainly sounds like you're on the right track." Then she paused and steeled herself. "Not for nothing, have either of you ever taken a DNA test?"

A look of delight crossed Nicole's face. "Not me, but my brother gave his dog a DNA test. He and his wife lived in a studio apartment and wanted a small pup. They saw an adorable little black-and-tan furball with a white chest and paws. The rescue folks said he was a miniature American shepherd that would grow to eighteen inches tall and maybe thirty pounds—exactly what they wanted. They named him Munchkin, but six months later he was so huge that they did the DNA thing. Turns out, he's an Anatolian shepherd/Great Pyrenees mix!"

"How big do they get?" Lonnie said.

"Let's just say he weighs more than my sister-in-law and eats off the kitchen counter."

Lonnie's eyes widened, and Maura winced.

"Well, it was just the catalyst they needed to move out of the city," explained Nicole, giggling. "I was able to help them find a house not far from here. Three years later, they have a lovely Cape with a big fenced-in backyard for Munchkin and an adorable baby girl for me to spoil. Best of all, I get to see them anytime I want. In the end, it was a win-win."

Maura chuckled. "I remember you talking about them moving to the area and then having your niece, but I never knew the backstory."

"What did we miss?" asked Josie as she and Kara approached the group. "What's so funny?"

Nicole quickly retold the story. It was just as humorous the second time.

"Why were you asking about DNA testing, Maura?" said Lonnie, ever the lawyer who stayed focused on details.

Maura now wished she hadn't brought up the topic, but the possibility of the test results bringing the past to the forefront was a threat she couldn't ignore.

"Well, the kids and I took a DNA test. They thought it would keep them connected to Paul. They see his DNA as his legacy, something he passed on to them that they can carry into the future."

"What a great idea," Nicole said. But Josie and Lonnie seemed to embrace Maura's original reaction, merely smiling and nodding their heads.

* * * * * * * * * * * * * *

Maura spent the rest of the day ticking items off her to-do list. As dinnertime neared, she sat down on the sofa, called Dean, and filled him in on her progress.

"You're off to a good start," he said. "I'm proud of you."

"Thank you, honey. I couldn't do it without your help, but I'm getting there."

"I'm going to have to run. Sam needs a ride to practice. I'll talk to you tomorrow."

Maura stood up, slid her phone into the back pocket of her jeans, and sauntered into the kitchen. She had been craving one of her and Paul's favorite dinners. It was a meal sophisticated enough to serve to company but quick and easy enough for a weeknight supper.

She gathered the ingredients on the kitchen island and began to assemble the dish of baked cod seasoned with pesto and a sprinkle of panko topping, along with roasted green beans tossed in olive oil with a squeeze of fresh lemon. It wasn't long before the pesto's earthy fragrance of garlic and basil filled the kitchen. When it was ready, she sat at the table with a chilled glass of sparkling water and a steaming plate of food. Even though her appetite had increased, more of the dinner than not ended up with the collection of leftovers in the freezer.

"A lot of good all that healthy eating did for Paul," she said aloud. "Swapping ground turkey for ground beef, eating fish two times a week, cutting back on carbs." Paul's father had passed away from a heart attack when he was only in his sixties. "Sometimes you can't escape DNA." She shook her head. The irony stung like rubbing alcohol on an open wound.

* * * * * * * * * * * * *

It was Friday night and a new tradition had begun. All family dinners were now held at Maura's place so that at the end of the night, she didn't have to drive home alone and enter an empty house. Everyone had decided that each family would rotate responsibility for the meal. It could be takeout or homemade, active or passive. Tonight was Maura's turn. Paul had always loved planning active meals, where guests participated in the making or assembling of the dish, so she decided to plan what Paul had called "fondue/fun do night." She prepared several fondue pots with various dippers.

The sun had reached a low point on the horizon as the family milled around the kitchen table, chatter filling the room. Armed with skewers, they took turns poking and dipping. There were three fondue pots. The first, filled with bubbling cheese, sat atop a platter of cubed ham, blanched carrots, and small boiled potatoes. Oil seasoned with anchovies, garlic, and red pepper flakes filled a second pot, which sat amidst a selection of crusty bread, cauliflower, and broccoli. The last, meant for dipping chicken and beef, contained a combination of vegetable stock, red wine, mushrooms, green onions, and garlic.

"Hey," Stephanie said between mouthfuls, "have either of you received an email confirming that your DNA kit is on its way to the lab?"

Dean nodded, and Maura explained that she hadn't checked her email in a few days. She picked up her phone and looked.

"Yes, it's right here," she answered as the now-familiar knot returned to her stomach.

"I almost forgot," shouted Sally, dropping her skewer, running to the family room, and returning with a bright-blue backpack dotted with unicorns. She unzipped the bag, reached deep inside, and pulled out a clear vinyl container of colored pencils. After placing them on the table, she plucked three red plastic rulers from her bag and set them next to the pencils. Finally, she retrieved a stack of worksheets, each containing two saucer-sized circles. One circle was labeled Dean, the other Stephanie.

"My class is working on pie graphs," Sally said. "But they're really just circles." She paused for a gulp of air. "Mom explained to me that Uncle Dean and her have Italian DNA from Pop, and Irish DNA from Gran, but we don't know how much they each got. I asked Mom if we could guess and show what we think in a pie graph."

Feeling her cheeks flush, Maura forced a grin. "That's a wonderful idea, pumpkin." She made her way over to Sally and gave her a hug.

"I bet mine will be the most accurate," proclaimed Jake, waving his skewer in the air like a victory flag.

"We'll see about that," countered Sam as he stabbed a hunk of bread with his fondue fork and swirled it through the gooey cheese mixture.

With the table cleared, Maura emerged from the kitchen with one last fondue pot filled with bubbling chocolate. Stephanie and Maddie followed behind carrying bowls piled high with strawberries, bananas, clementines, and cubes of pound cake. The poking and dipping continued as everyone set to work on the pie graphs.

"Can I have a ruler?" asked Sam.

"I need some colored pencils," said Jake.

"These clementine slices taste amazing dipped in chocolate," said Stephanie. "Try one, Kyle."

Dean glanced over at Sam's worksheet. "Are you sure about that, buddy? I think you're off-base with Aunt Stephanie's graph."

Sam grimaced playfully and turned to Maddie. "Mom, tell Dad to mind his own business!"

The teasing continued as each person made the case for their choices, small squabbles erupting sporadically; however, one thing they all agreed on was that the chocolate fondue was the best pot of the night.

When she had finished dessert, Sally collected the graphs and attached them to the fridge with a magnet clip. "Mom, this was wonderful. Thanks so much." Everyone agreed, and Stephanie hugged her mother goodbye.

"You're all welcome," Maura said, "and thank you again for the pie graphs, Sally." She leaned over and planted a kiss on top of Sally's head.

"We've got next week's meal," announced Maddie as the crowd headed toward the door.

"I wish we'd started this a long time ago," said Sam.

Dean put his arm around his son. "We all do, buddy."

The house empty, Maura returned to the kitchen. She made a cup of chamomile tea, unclipped the charts, and rifled through the stack. When she was through, she reattached them to the fridge and stood frozen, her eyes distant, her head rotating from side to side. Lost deep in thought, her body became rigid at the sound of her mug smashing on the tile floor.

CHAPTER 4

"The trouble is you think you have time."

— *Gautama Buddha*

The stately antique grandfather clock in the foyer chimed ten times as Maura stood next to her bed, her gym bag resting on top of the billowy white comforter. She reached into the center section of the bag, pulled out her sweaty workout clothes, and dropped them in the clothes hamper tucked in the corner. Plunging her hand in again, she retrieved her sneakers, then walked to the closet and placed them on the wire shoe rack attached to the wall. She caught a glimpse of a pair of purple suede stilettos. Their thin ankle straps, dangling alongside the frayed sneaker shoelace, sparked a memory.

The purple pumps hadn't seen the light of day since last June, during Dean and Maddie's twentieth-wedding-anniversary party. As the entire family watched, Paul had spun Maura across the dance floor. And then there was the moment the DJ had handed Stephanie the karaoke microphone. As usual, she'd stolen the show.

A feeling of dread sprouted up from Maura's gut and landed in her chest. Oh, how she longed for things to return to the way they were. Even if she and Paul hadn't been perfect, at least they'd been predictable. She curled up on the closet floor, hugging her knees until her angst subsided.

Returning to her bedside, she reached her hand into one of the side pockets of her gym bag—not the one with the mesh top, where she kept her toiletries, but the other one, where she stored miscellaneous items. It was filled with protein bar wrappers, empty water bottles, hair ties, a pen, two crumpled receipts from the club cafe, and a business card. She read the bold red print: IT'S ABOUT TIME. Staring at the card, she wondered why it hadn't occurred to her sooner: She would invite The Coastal Club girls out of the locker room and over to her house for dinner. *If anyone can help me navigate what's to come, it will be them.*

On Monday, Maura arrived at the gym at 5:45 a.m., a bit later than usual. Having missed the start of Extreme Boot Camp, she entered the fitness room for a TRX full-body suspension workout, coupled with sprints on the treadmill. At the TRX station, she approached the recognizable black-and-bright-yellow straps hanging from hooks in the ceiling. She selected one, gripped the stirrup-like handles, and kept the straps taut as she moved through a series of exercises. After thirty minutes of squatting, lunging, and planking in various progressions, she moved onto the treadmill. Half an hour later, she'd had enough. The TRX workout always made her body feel strong yet flexible, and the sprints provided the endorphin rush she craved.

Back in the locker room, she gathered the girls together. "I know this is uncharted territory for us," she said, "but I was wondering if you'd all like to come over for dinner on Wednesday night. We could share some food and wine and have an unhurried conversation for a change. I've been cooking up a storm, and between that and the food I accumulated after Paul's funeral, I have a freezer full of entrees."

There was a five-second delay, and then all at once, everyone chimed in.

"I'd love to," said Josie.

"What can I bring?" asked Kara.

"Count me in," added Lonnie.

"I'm down for that," exclaimed Nicole.

They planned to arrive at Maura's house at six thirty on Wednesday and left the locker room seeming excited about the next phase of their friendship.

* * * * * * * * * * * * *

Kara arrived on the dot. "Woo-hoo!" she called from the foyer after letting herself in. She entered the kitchen and gave Maura a warm hug. "Oh good! Since I brought the appetizer, I'm glad I'm the first one here. It's a vegetable platter with hummus. I don't want to sabotage Lonnie. Where do you want it?"

"Family room works," said Maura.

"Okay, I'll put it on the coffee table."

Involuntarily, Maura's hand shot to her throat.

"Oh no, I'm so sorry!" said Kara.

"It's okay. You've just confirmed the fact that it's time to shop for a new coffee table. Want to go furniture shopping this weekend?"

"I'd love to. You know I never pass up a chance to shop!" Kara headed to the family room and set her platter on a side table.

"I'll get it," Kara called after the doorbell sounded. She trotted to the foyer as the last bit of sunlight streamed through the transom above. Then she pulled open the door to find Lonnie, Nicole, and Josie. "Come on in, let me take your coats." She pointed down the hall. "Maura is in the kitchen."

"Hello, Maura," shouted Nicole as she meandered down the narrow hall with its thick white moldings. "What a beautiful neighborhood!" She made a sweeping gesture with her hand. "And this kitchen is fabulous." She turned to Josie and Lonnie. "Just look at these industrial appliances."

"Hi, everyone!" Maura said. "Thanks, Nicole. As I'm sure you recall, a few years ago we updated the kitchen and never regretted it."

"How could we forget," chimed in Kara. "You agonized over the cabinets. I remember Paul wanted cherry wood and you wanted white."

"I'm glad you won that battle," Nicole said. "The cabinets are gorgeous. And wasn't there a flooring debate? You wanted hardwoods and Paul wanted tile."

"And since you picked the cabinets, he picked the floor," added Lonnie with a chuckle.

"Your table looks so pretty," Josie said.

The table was dressed with gleaming white plates atop bright-yellow placemats. A yellow-and-white-checked napkin in a thin silver napkin ring adorned each plate. In the center of the table rested a clear, round, cantaloupe-sized bowl with a mixture of pale and bright-yellow daffodils spilling over the sides.

"Regardless of everything else, I'm determined to acknowledge spring," said Maura, a tinge of sorrow coloring her cheeks pink. "Who's ready for a glass of wine?" She turned to Josie and Nicole. "Girls, grab the wine and follow me."

She pointed the group toward the family room. The wine was poured, and snack plates were filled. The guests sank into the oversized moss-colored sofa, where the cushions practically screamed, *Couch potatoes welcome!* Maura settled onto the adjacent green leather recliner.

"I propose a toast to Maura," said Nicole, "for transporting us out of the locker room and into the world beyond."

"To Maura," cried Lonnie as each woman raised her glass.

"It's crazy, isn't it?" Maura said. "We've been friends for so long. Actually, Lonnie, it was your trainer's business card that made it clear we needed to spend some time together out of the locker room."

"It's about time!" they said in unison.

For the next hour, they reminisced about the milestones and struggles they'd shared in locker room conversations. They'd reported on birthdays, graduations, and anniversaries. They'd discussed relationship struggles between partners, family members, and co-workers. And they'd celebrated promotions, goals, and simple pleasures.

"Who's ready to eat?" Maura said, smiling. "Refill your glasses and meet me in the kitchen."

In the kitchen, Maura directed them to grab plates and head to the center island, where an array of aluminum trays covered the granite countertop: the pesto-and-breadcrumb-crusted fish dinner from last week; lemon chicken with a side of deep-green sautéed broccoli rabe and baby potatoes; pink salmon topped with mango salsa, brown rice, and bright-orange baby carrots; and steamed tofu, zucchini, eggplant, black olives and pungent Spanish onions in a balsamic glaze atop an array of trivets. They all blended together to create a bouquet of aromas and colors.

The women filled their plates and found seats at the table, and the conversation picked up where it had left off until Maura steered the topic back to the present. "I don't mean to put a damper on the night, but I'm a little concerned about Dean. I think he's having a difficult time with Paul's death."

"How so?" asked Kara.

"Paul was always his sounding board and biggest supporter. I'm afraid his dad's death has left quite a void in Dean's life." She paused, her eyebrows knitting together. "Dean is a fixer, and he always has a hard time accepting that there are some things he just can't fix."

"Maybe one of the bereavement counselors I sent you could be of help," said Josie.

"I agree, but every time I suggest that, he changes the subject."

"Keep the lines of communication open," Josie said. "And give it some time."

"How is Stephanie making out?" asked Kara.

"She seems to be managing. Stephanie's always been the more flexible of the two. When they were young, on the last day of school, Stephanie would bound off the bus and skip into the house, ready for the first adventure of summer to begin. Dean, on the other hand, would drag his backpack across the yard, head hung low, and then plop himself down and sulk. He's never liked change; I think it makes him feel a loss of control."

"It's amazing how different siblings can be," said Kara.

"Isn't that the truth," said Maura, her thoughts suddenly ricocheting to the DNA test.

When they'd all had their fill of food and chatter, they worked together and cleaned the kitchen in no time. Kara retrieved their coats, and they all agreed that the conversation was wonderful and the food outstanding.

"Lonnie, I loved your dessert," Nicole said while buttoning her faded jean jacket. "And Maura, you could cook professionally."

"Agreed," said Lonnie. "Have you ever thought of branching out of your kitchen?"

"You flatter me!" said Maura as she clapped her hand to her chest, fingers spread wide. "Would you all be willing to come back next week? I really find cooking therapeutic, and I'd love you to help me eat my leftovers."

"We'll form a supper club!" said Nicole.

"Perfect," Josie said, "but I propose that every fourth supper club, we take Maura out and treat her to dinner."

After they left, Maura latched the lock and swept through the downstairs rooms, turning off the lights. She climbed the stairs and entered the bedroom before spying the trainer's business card on her dresser. It seemed to scream at her anew: IT'S ABOUT TIME!

"Which I'm running out of," she lamented as she changed into her pajamas and climbed into bed.

CHAPTER 5

"It does not matter how slowly you go as long as you do not stop."

– Confucius

Ever since Paul's death, Maura's sense of time had become elusive. One day would pass in a flurry of phone calls and the filling out of endless forms, while the next would find her staring at the ceiling, her mind creating a plethora of scenarios around the potential results of the DNA test. *What might it reveal to Dean and Stephanie? How would it impact her own future?*

By Friday night, she found it hard to believe that another week had passed. Once again—and much to her delight—the family assembled around her farm table for dinner. Maddie had made lasagna, and everyone dug in.

Halfway through the meal, Sally cleared her throat loudly and addressed the family. "Can we tell stories about Pop tonight? Mom says if we tell stories about someone we miss, it can make it seem like they're still here."

"That's a wonderful idea, Sally," said Maura.

The first story was set around a cruise the family took to celebrate Paul's sixtieth birthday. Laughter broke out as Stephanie recounted the final dinner of the trip. As the waitstaff had danced in a conga line, the diners had stood and clapped along. Suddenly, Sally had climbed onto her chair and twirled a linen napkin over her head as she swayed to the beat of the music. Sally said she didn't know what had gotten into her, though she remembered Paul joking that perhaps her Shirley Temple had been spiked!

Maura passed the salad bowl to Kyle, and Dean followed with a story of his own about a father-son outing back when he was in middle school. Paul used to take Dean and a few of his friends on an overnight excursion once each summer during those years. His story about a camping expedition to find the Jersey Devil ended just as Jake beat Sally out for the last piece of garlic bread.

Sam then left the table and returned with a box that had originally housed a case of wine but was now home to a pile of DVDs.

"Gran, can we watch some home movies?"

"Absolutely," Maura said. "You hook up the player. Jake and Sally, pick out some DVDs for us to watch. We'll clean up dinner while you get set up."

It wasn't long before everyone was gathered around the television. They howled with laughter over Paul's shaky videotaping job of Stephanie's college graduation; the camera was so jumpy, Maura almost got nauseous watching it. But when Paul filled the screen—reading one of his infamous poems at Christmas dinner—you could hear a pin drop. Throughout the next hour, tears of joy and sorrow were spilled. Overall, Maura felt it was a cathartic experience for everyone.

"That's enough for one night," Maura said as Sally handed Sam another DVD. "It's getting late."

With another Friday night dinner in the books, everyone gathered their things and headed out the door.

As Stephanie walked to the car, she called back to her mother. "In case you haven't checked, we got emails today from the DNA company. Kits are in the lab, and results should be ready in four weeks."

"Four weeks," whined Sally as she climbed into the car. "That's forever!"

Maura felt the hairs on the back of her neck stand on end.

* * * * * * * * * * * * * *

On Saturday morning, Maura and Kara wandered around their favorite furniture store, looking for something casual yet traditional, a reflection of Maura's decorating style. But no luck. After four hours and three more stores, Maura finally saw something that would work: a leather ottoman in cinnamon that would complement the decor. Best of all, it had a removable lid for storage. When the grandkids stayed overnight, they often played games; now she could store them in the ottoman and free up the coat-closet shelf.

Maura's thoughts jumped to Paul. She remembered a night, shortly after Dean's first birthday, when she and Paul had looked forward to a stay-at-home date…

"Get over here, you sexy thing," Paul said as Maura entered

the family room in a black lace teddy.

"Shh!" she said, drawing a finger to her lips and smiling. "Don't wake the baby."

"I'm sorry, babe, but you look amazing."

"Oh, Paul," she cooed, "I don't ever think I've been this happy."

Paul moved toward her and hooked a pinky finger under each of the spaghetti straps of her camisole, slowly sliding them over her shoulders before leaning down and devouring her with his kiss. They made love that night in the family room, casting their clothes onto the coffee table.

Maura flinched at the sound of the saleswoman's voice. "Here you go ma'am, you're all set. I have your credit card and receipt. Give the store a call Monday to arrange Tuesday's delivery."

Maura fumbled with the receipt and credit card, shoving them into her nylon shoulder tote.

"It's been a pleasure doing business with you," said the saleswoman. "You've made a good selection today. That piece will probably outlast you!"

Maura smirked at the absurdity of the remark.

"How about lunch?" suggested Kara as they exited the showroom. "Shopping always makes me ravenous."

"Let's go!"

At a quaint old pub in town, they sat at a high-top table for two next to a quirky hexagonal window. The dimly lit room seemed to invite heartfelt conversation.

"I still can't believe it," said Maura as she pierced a cherry tomato with her fork. "I mean, today I bought a new coffee table because the old one was broken by Paul falling to his death. How can that be?" She frowned, deep parallel lines forming between her brows. "No one lives forever, but I never expected to be on my own so soon. You create a life and you think you have all the bases covered, then you're thrown a curveball." She took a sip of her chardonnay. "Family aside, I don't know how I could get through this without you."

Kara reached across the table and squeezed her friend's hand. "Come on, let's finish up, then grab a coffee and window-shop before we head home."

Welcoming the distraction, Maura agreed. "I'd love to."

It was not until later, when she pulled her car into the empty garage, that the finality of Paul's death knocked the wind out of her once more.

CHAPTER 6

"You never know when the truth
will come home.
You can't choose the time.
The time chooses you."

— Rick Yancey, The Infinite Sea

Maura took a seat at the small kitchen desk that was flanked by matching pantry cabinets. Paying bills and sorting through financial statements had become part of her new routine. When she finished, she gathered her papers and slid them into a folder, which she placed in one of the cubbies above. Until recently, the desktop had housed an assortment of family pictures in glossy white wooden frames of varying sizes, and the cubbies had displayed the spines of Maura and Paul's favorite cookbooks. Now it served as her workspace.

It was time to prepare what had been deemed the "Supper Club" dinner, and this Wednesday, she was ready to share not only her delectable dinner but her dilemma as well. The stack of aluminum tins was shrinking, but there was still plenty to choose from. She randomly selected four frozen entrees and deposited them on the kitchen island's beige-and-black-speckled countertop. Then she tossed together a salad and set the table while the oven preheated. It wasn't long before the tins were warming and the prep work was done.

By six forty-five, the women had assembled at Maura's house.

"I love the new ottoman," said Nicole as she entered the family room.

Maura immediately felt as if the floor had shifted. She was becoming accustomed to pangs of grief catching her off-balance, so she rebounded quickly. "Thanks. Kara helped me pick it out last weekend."

Soon enough, the women settled in and caught each other up on the latest Coastal Club happenings.

"Did anyone check out that new trainer?" asked Nicole. "He is so hot!"

"Didn't you learn your lesson the last time you had your eye on a new trainer?" Kara asked as she ran a baby carrot through Lonnie's low-fat dip. "You hurt your back lifting because you were trying to impress what's-his-name, and you ended up in the chiropractor's office."

"I know, I know. This time, I'll work out *next* to the new guy, not with him."

Maura got up and refilled her wine glass. "Ladies, I need your advice." She returned and gulped down a mouthful of pinot grigio.

"What is it?" asked Nicole.

"You're not sick, are you?" asked Josie.

Maura shook her head. "No, I'm fine."

"Did something happen to one of the kids?" asked Kara.

Maura reached for the thick mane bundled at the nape of her neck and ran her hand along the length of her ponytail. "Do you remember I told you that Stephanie, Dean, and I took a DNA test?"

"Yeah, and I told you the story about my brother's dog," said Nicole as a grin spread across her face.

"Well, the results should be available in about four weeks."

"And?" asked Lonnie.

"There's a potential problem," Maura said, taking another swig of wine. "It has to do with Paul."

The women gazed at Maura and edged forward in their seats.

"He had a high school sweetheart. Her name was Lisa. They started dating their sophomore year." Maura cleared her throat before continuing. "When they were juniors, she got pregnant."

"Oh boy," said Nicole as she got up to refill her wine glass.

"Paul went to an all-boys Catholic school, and Lisa went to an all-girls, so abortion was not an option." She turned to Nicole. "Back then, when a girl became pregnant, the parents took her out of school. Lucky for Lisa, the nuns were nurturing, tutoring her when she could no longer attend classes. Anyway, the summer before her senior year, Lisa gave birth to a baby girl and named her Anna.

"As you can imagine, senior year was not what Paul or Lisa had planned, but they made the best of it. Paul continued playing sports; he was a three-season varsity athlete. Lisa was no longer the head cheerleader, but she was able to graduate on time with the rest of the class."

Maura realized she had been squeezing her knitted fingers, so she relaxed her grasp and took another swallow of wine.

"Although nothing was formally agreed upon, Paul's family provided some support for the baby, but Lisa and her parents were the primary caregivers for Anna. Paul would spend Sunday afternoons with Lisa and the baby whenever he wasn't working at his father's gas station, but during the week, he was busy with school, practice, and games."

The women sat frozen as they listened.

"When Paul got accepted to Penn State, it was a big deal. He was an only child, and the family's aspirations rested on his shoulders. He explained to Lisa that he would come home on weekends, and off he went. She stayed behind, got a secretarial job at a law firm, and went about raising Anna.

"As time went on, Paul became entrenched in college life, and he visited Lisa and the baby less and less. Lisa began a relationship with an auto-parts salesman, and they eventually married. Paul didn't object when Lisa's new husband offered to adopt Anna. He trusted in the fact that she would be raised in a stable home. He wasn't ready to settle down and still had several years of school in front of him, so he moved on.

"By the time I met him in graduate school, Lisa and the baby were a distant memory. When we became serious, he told me the story. He made it clear that he felt it was best for Anna if he stayed out of her life. He said it would be less complicated for her, and I supported his wishes." Maura sighed deeply. "After I gave birth to Dean, Paul held him for the first time and wept uncontrollably. I always felt he was crying for Anna, but after initially telling me her story, he'd never wanted to discuss her again, so I don't know for sure." She paused. "Paul was a wonderful father to both Stephanie and Dean. They adored him and put him on a pedestal." A tear slid down her cheek.

Lonnie handed Maura a cocktail napkin. "And now you're afraid that the DNA test will reveal Anna as Dean and Stephanie's half-sister."

Maura closed her eyes and nodded slowly. Then she opened them and gazed into the distance. "If Anna has ever taken a DNA test, her results will be in the system." The cadence of her voice picked up speed. "Dean and Stephanie will be devastated. They won't understand why they were never told about her. Dean is struggling already, and I'm afraid he won't be able to cope."

"What are you going to do?" asked Nicole.

She looked at her friends, searching for a lifeline. "I don't know. I was hoping all of you could help me figure that out."

"Maura, I've known Dean and Stephanie since they were born," said Kara. "They are both very reasonable. I'm sure that after you explain everything, they'll understand that it was Paul's decision to keep the past in the past."

"I've said it before, and I'll say it again," said Josie. "A family counselor could be a great help at a time like this."

"The sooner you tell them the truth, the better," said Lonnie. "This information should come from you, not from test results. More importantly, you don't want this information coming from Paul's daughter at some point in the future."

"I think Lonnie's right. Dean and Stephanie need to hear this from you," said Josie.

"I agree," said Kara.

"Okay, okay, I hear you," said Maura, her wine glass teetering as she placed it on the side table with a trembling hand.

CHAPTER 7

"Embrace uncertainty.
Some of the most beautiful chapters in our lives won't have a title until much later."

– Bob Goff

Sally burst through Maura's front door as the grandfather clock struck six. "Gran? Where are you?"

"I'm in the kitchen."

"Guess what we're having for dinner!" Sally exclaimed as she galloped down the hall toward the sound of her grandmother's voice. "It's my favorite."

"Then it must be your dad's famous barbecued ribs," said Maura as she bent down to hug Sally.

Stephanie and Kyle enjoyed cooking together as much as Maura and Paul had, and tonight it was their turn to supply the family dinner. They entered the kitchen moments after Sally, carrying Kyle's sweet-and-tangy grilled ribs and Stephanie's homemade potato salad.

Throughout the meal, Maura did her best to focus on the food and conversation, but save for the sticky barbecue sauce coating her fingertips, she was barely aware of what she was eating.

With full bellies, the cousins retreated to the family room while the adults cleaned.

"I love the new look, Mom," said Stephanie when the adults joined the children. "What do you think, Dean?"

"I'll get used to it," he mumbled as he slid the top off the ottoman to investigate its contents.

"Anyone up for a game?" asked Jake, nudging aside his uncle and pulling out a black box with bold white letters.

After dividing the family into two teams, a robust game of Pictionary ensued until a winning team was crowned. Everyone was still throwing barbs at each other as they piled out the door.

"Stephanie! Dean!" Maura called from the front porch. "Do you think you could come by tomorrow afternoon? I'd like to talk to you about something."

* * * * * * * * * * * * * *

On Saturday afternoon, shortly after three o'clock, Stephanie and Dean arrived at their childhood home. Maura led them to the kitchen, where fresh-baked chocolate chip cookies and a steaming pot of coffee awaited. After filling three mugs, Maura gestured for them to sit down.

"What's up, Mom?" asked Dean.

"It has to do with the DNA kits," said Maura.

"Did you get your results?" asked Stephanie excitedly.

"No, but there is some DNA information I have to share with you both. This should have been done long before now, but your father preferred to keep you out of it."

"What is it?" asked Stephanie, grinning. "Do I have the sister I always begged for?"

Maura sighed.

"Mom, just tell us," said Dean. "Are we not Italian—and our name is really Shipkowski?" He winked at Stephanie.

"Promise you'll hear me out. I have a story to tell you." Maura locked eyes first with Stephanie and then turned her gaze to Dean. "Promise."

"Of course," replied Dean as a look of concern crept across his face. Stephanie nodded in agreement.

Maura recounted how she and Paul had met during graduate school in the library, studying for exams. They'd been sitting at adjacent desks in the stacks—the upper level of the library—where talking was prohibited. Paul had written corny jokes and passed them to Maura. At one point, they'd both burst out laughing and had been asked to leave. As they rode the elevator down to the library lobby, Paul had asked Maura to go out for a pizza, and from that point on, they'd remained inseparable.

"I love that story," Stephanie said dreamily.

"Well, there's one you haven't heard," said Maura, and she told the story of Paul, Lisa, and Anna. When she finished, the three of them sat in silence for what seemed an eternity.

Dean spoke first. "What exactly do you want us to do with this information?" Head down, he stared at the table, his foot tapping the floor at an ever-increasing speed, like a time bomb ready to explode. Suddenly, he raised his head and turned to Maura, his eyes wide with rage. "Oh, I get it—you're afraid she might show up on the DNA results, so you had to tell us about her." He dropped his head again, turning it slowly from left to right. "This is unbelievable!"

It was as if a floodgate had opened, and all of Dean's pent-up emotions from Paul's death rushed out. "How could Dad keep this from us? I idolized him my whole life. Now I don't even know who he was." He jumped up from his chair, nearly toppling it. "I can't deal with this right now. I have to go." He stormed from the house.

Stephanie slowly pushed her chair away from the table, tears streaming down her face. "Mom, how could you keep this from us? You're a fraud, no better than Dad." She glared at Maura, her steel-gray eyes cutting like a knife. "I have to go too. I need to process this." As if in a trance, she shuffled toward the front door, closing it gently behind her.

Alone at the table, Maura stared at the half-eaten plate of cookies and empty coffee cups, the only proof that the conversation had actually taken place. She seethed. *After all these years, I'm left to clean up this mess!* For the first time since Paul's death, she felt angry.

* * * * * * * * * * * * *

Maura awoke in a tangle of covers, anxious to hit the gym. She couldn't wait to lose herself in a workout.

Once there, her anger at Paul fueled her through the Extreme Boot Camp warm-up, but midway through class, somewhere between goblet squats, renegade rows, and a grid of bear-crawls and gorillas, her anger transformed into energy. By the time the cooldown began, her angst flushed through her pores and drowned in a small pool of sweat, which she wiped away with a towel.

"I can't believe it; I've lost five more pounds," said Lonnie as she stepped off the scale in the far corner of the locker room.

"Good for you," called Kara from her locker bay.

"We're so proud of you," added Maura as she stepped away from her locker and moved toward Lonnie.

"What are we proud of?" asked Nicole as she and Josie rounded the corner.

"Lonnie lost five more pounds," said Maura.

"You really are serious this time," said Josie while Nicole clapped her hands and grinned.

"I am," said Lonnie. "My nutrition coach and trainer want me to slow down, but I'm on a mission. I feel really good." Then she chuckled and rubbed her quads. "Sore, but good."

"Maybe you'll take an aqua class with me," Josie said. "They're great for cardio and toning."

"That would mean I'd have to get into a bathing suit!"

"Well, in the words of Eleanor Roosevelt, 'Do one thing every day that scares you.'"

"Me in a bathing suit?" Lonnie cackled. "I'm more worried about scaring everyone else. Besides, I don't like to get my hair wet."

Josie laughed. "Neither do half the women in the class!"

"Enough about me," Lonnie said. "Maura, how did you make out talking with your kids?"

The group huddled closer as Maura relayed the emotional scene in her kitchen. "I haven't heard from either of them yet," she finished, shrugging. "To be honest, the entire situation has left me feeling so angry at Paul." With a puff, she blew back a stray strand of hair. "I know a vigorous workout helps me deal, but an endorphin rush only lasts so long, and this morning's is wearing off already."

CHAPTER 8

Time flies over us
but leaves its shadow behind.

— *Nathaniel Hawthorne*

Ancient oak trees lined the street, their branches creating a canopy. An inviting front porch with intricately carved gingerbread trim welcomed clients to the counseling center. Maura climbed the worn wooden stairs as a wind chime tingled in the brisk April breeze and helped to create a warm vibe.

Maura pushed open a heavy mahogany door and was greeted by a woman in a '60s-inspired peasant skirt—or was it vintage? Her salt-and-pepper curls rested on her shoulders. "It's so nice to meet you," the woman said in a voice that evoked images of dripping honey. "I'm Lydia." She gestured toward the next room. "Please, have a seat."

"Thanks. I'm a little uneasy. I've never met with a

therapist." The cream-colored room contained a small but ornate fireplace flanked by two wingback chairs on one side and a love seat on the other. An antique coffee table rested in the center. It reminded Maura of the dollhouse Santa had brought Stephanie when she was eight.

"I understand," said Lydia.

"Does it matter where I sit?"

"Wherever you're comfortable."

Maura settled on the love seat, leaving Lydia her choice of wingback chair.

"Would you like some water?" Lydia asked, pointing out the crystal water pitcher and two glasses on the table.

"No thanks, I'm fine."

"On the phone, you told me your husband recently passed away. I'm so sorry for your loss."

"Thank you." Maura's lips curved into a lopsided smile.

"Can you tell me about that?"

Maura shared the events of Paul's death and the request by her children to take a DNA test.

"You've had a lot to deal with these past few weeks," said Lydia. "How are you feeling now?"

Maura's cheeks tingled. "Recently, angry."

"Do you know why?"

Maura disclosed the story of Paul's past. She rationalized the decision to keep the secret from the children all these years and described how and why she recently told them the truth. Finally, she shared how alone she felt because she hadn't heard from either of them since.

"Give them time. They have a lot to process. You said they're close. More than likely, they're sorting things out together. I'd like to focus on you now. Finish this sentence: I am angry at Paul for…"

Maura felt her fingernails digging into her palms. "I am angry at Paul for leaving me to deal with all of this."

"And again. I am angry at Paul for…"

"I am angry at him for being irresponsible and having a child out of wedlock," she said, her voice cracking.

"I am angry at Paul for…"

"I am so angry at Paul for dying!" Maura began to whimper. Her whimper turned into a heaving sob.

Lydia gestured to the tissues. "On my count, I want you to inhale. One, two, three."

Maura sat up and inhaled a gulp of air.

"Now exhale. One, two, three."

She released the breath with a snort.

"Again, inhale."

This time, Maura filled her belly with air as she silently counted along with Lydia.

"Now exhale. One, two, three."

After repeating the breathing exercise two more times, Maura pulled a tissue from the box and brought it to her nose. She grabbed another and dabbed her eyes.

"Now listen to me," said Lydia. "What I hear you saying is that you've already lost your husband and now you are afraid you will lose your children. Is that true?"

Tears pooled in Maura's eyes, but this time she was able to keep them from spilling down her cheeks. "Yes," she said quietly.

"Maura, you described a family with healthy, loving relationships. I'm not here to judge the way you and Paul handled the situation with his firstborn, but I am here to remind you that as a loving wife, you agreed to support Paul's decision. Now as a loving mother, all you can do is support your children while they try to make sense of this, and then support their decision about how they want to handle the relationship with their half-sister."

They talked for a while longer before agreeing to meet again the following Wednesday.

"Please don't hesitate to reach out sooner if you feel the need," said Lydia.

"Thanks, but I hope I won't have to." A grin lit up her face. "No offense."

* * * * * * * * * * * * *

A doorbell chime startled Maura awake. A purplish glow blanketed the room as she scanned her surroundings to get her bearings. The events of the counseling session came rushing back as she turned on the lamp next to the couch. She glanced at her Smartwatch and was surprised to see it was 6:25 p.m.

"Coming," she called as she jumped up and jogged into the foyer. She pulled open the door and found Josie on the porch with a bottle of wine in hand.

"Oh my gosh, come in," said Maura, her angled eyebrows arching high. "I haven't got anything ready. I came home from my therapy session and sat down for a moment; I must have passed out!" She led Josie to the kitchen

"That's not unusual. Therapy can be stressful. But right now, tell me what I can do to help."

Maura gestured to the island. "If you could fill that ice bucket and bring these snack plates and napkins into the family room, I'll pop the entrees into the oven." Maura pulled trays from the freezer and set them on the stovetop.

"How did—" Before Josie could finish, the doorbell chimed, and a voice rang out from the foyer.

"Hello!" called Kara as she entered the kitchen with Lonnie and Nicole trailing behind. "We come bearing snacks, desserts, wine, and gossip."

"Hi, everyone," cried Maura. "I was just telling Josie that I fell asleep after therapy and didn't wake up until she rang the doorbell."

"Did you find a fit with a counselor I suggested?" Josie asked immediately.

"Yes, I met with Lydia. I felt really comfortable talking with her." Maura slid a final tin into the oven, then crossed her arms across her chest. "She suggested I give the kids time, but I'll tell you, this is all so difficult."

Josie stepped forward and gave her a hug. It took only a moment for the others to join in.

"Okay, ladies," said Nicole as they disengaged, "let's get this show on the road. It's time for a supper club therapy session!"

With everyone situated in the family room, Nicole shared her most recent dating debacle. "I really liked his profile, not to mention his picture. We went back and forth online a few times. He was funny and seemed smart, so we decided to meet at a bar thirty minutes from here—a halfway point for both of us. I was really excited." She sipped her wine. "But I got held up in traffic, and by the time I got there, maybe twenty minutes late, he was already wasted. The next thing I know, he's moving his barstool closer to mine, putting his hand on my thigh, and squeezing my knee, so I excused myself to the bathroom and hightailed it out of there! I'm about to give up on ever finding a man."

"Nicole, you crack me up," said Kara. "How about you, Lonnie? I haven't heard you mention anyone since you and Dan broke up."

"Oh no, right now I'm focusing on me," said Lonnie.

"Excuse me, ladies," Maura said, "but it smells like our dinner may be ready. Shall we dine?"

Plates and wine glasses were filled as banter about the gym and its members continued throughout the meal.

"Well, girls," announced Josie, "I don't know about you, but my alarm is going off early tomorrow."

Maura was still giggling as she shut the front door. *Mindless chatter—what a perfect way to end the day.*

She climbed the stairs, entered her bedroom, and slipped out of the denim skirt she'd been wearing all day. Then she walked into the master bathroom. Maura and Paul had lived in this house for thirty-five years. They loved it, but in addition to the small closet, the bathroom had driven them crazy. It housed a single sink and a tiny stand-up shower stall.

Maura sighed longingly. She gazed heavenward and spoke aloud. "You know what, Paul? Regardless of this anger eating away at me, I'd give anything to be bumping into you right now as we try to brush our teeth at the same time."

She climbed into bed and stared at the ceiling. The house seemed quieter than usual, and she felt more alone than she'd ever thought possible.

CHAPTER 9

"I walk slowly,
but I never walk backward."

— *Unknown*

Maura picked up the steel ladle from the ceramic spoon rest and stirred the minestrone soup warming on the stove. Concerns swirled around her brain like the beans and pasta spinning in the pot. *What if no one shows up for family dinner tonight? What if Dean and Stephanie won't forgive me? What if they decide to reach out to Anna? What if Anna wants nothing to do with them? What if she does? What if she resents that Dean and Stephanie were raised by Paul, and she wasn't?*

She pulled a platter of sandwiches from the fridge and placed it on the kitchen island, then sat at the table and waited. It was nearly seven before the front door opened.

"Hi, Mom," called Stephanie. "It's only me and Dean tonight," she explained as they made their way to the kitchen.

"We decided to come by ourselves so we could talk about Anna some more."

Maura rose to greet them. "I understand."

"Do you, Mom?" said Dean, raising his voice as he took a beer from the fridge. "Do you understand how this has rocked our world?"

"Dean, don't yell at Mom." Stephanie turned to Maura. "It's just that we don't understand how you could have made the decision to keep this from us all these years."

"It wasn't my decision to make. It was my job to support your father and his wishes, in the same way I'll support yours now."

"He abandoned his own flesh and blood," Dean said, his eyes filling with tears. "Who does that? Who was he?"

Maura pulled a chair away from the head of the table and sat down. "He was a man, Dean. He was a man doing the best he could, just like we all are. I'm not here to defend him, but I do know that he was young and under immense pressure from home to move on with his life." She leaned forward in her chair. "People make mistakes, Dean!" As an overwhelming feeling of despair swallowed her, she covered her face and sobbed.

Dean moved toward her, then got down on his knees and hugged her. "I'm sorry, Mom. Please don't cry."

Maura squeezed the water from her eyes, then sat erect and placed her hands on her thighs. "You're right. I don't know what it's like to lose a father and then learn you have a half-sister, all in such a short period of time, but I do know that if we focus on blame and anger, and question what we know to be true, it will destroy us. We are a family and there is nothing we can't work through. I love you both so much. You two are all I have."

"We love you too, Mom," said Stephanie, "but that's not the point. Dean and I have been talking. This just makes us question everything we thought we knew about Dad, and we have to figure out how to deal with Anna. I mean, I've always wanted a sister, and now I find out that I actually have one. It feels insane!"

Dean snorted loudly. "I don't want to talk about that yet. I'm still stuck on the fact that Dad kept something so monumental from us. Every time I look at Sam, I wonder how Dad could have written off his child."

"All I can tell you is that regardless of what your father decided, you should never question his love for you."

"I know," agreed Stephanie, "and I'm sorry I called you a fraud for sticking by Dad. If Kyle and I were in this situation, I would have done the same as you."

Maura reached out and squeezed Stephanie's fingers. Without releasing her grip, she slid her other hand across the table and grasped Dean's hand. "Promise me that you will keep the lines of communication open as you decide together how to move forward. I don't want us to lose any more than we already have, and maybe we can gain something in this process."

As they sat in silence, Maura sensed they could all navigate this journey together.

"Can we put this conversation to rest for tonight?" asked Dean. He took a swig of his beer. "I don't know about you, but I'm starving."

"Me too," said Stephanie.

For the next hour, life almost felt normal as they ate, drank, listened, and laughed—and family ties tightened once again.

CHAPTER 10

Time is the wisest counselor of all.

— Pericles

"So, fill me in on yesterday," said Maura as she and Kara pedaled into town.

Kara didn't hesitate to report on the Freaky Friday hijinks. "The kids looked adorable in their mismatched outfits. They had so much fun. Instead of a regular math lesson, we did math puzzles, and during science, they worked in groups on a surprise experiment using ice and rock salt."

"Did they roll coffee cans back and forth for about twenty minutes?"

"You bet, and were they ever surprised when they removed the lids and found ice cream inside! We did Mad Libs too, and they had a great time."

"Sounds like you did too."

They slid their pastel-colored cruisers—the bicycle of

choice at the Jersey Shore—into a rack near the center of town.

"I thought we'd go to Sprouts and Such for lunch," Kara said. "What do you think?"

"Let's do it."

While awaiting their orders, they sipped berry-infused iced tea in the small dining area filled mostly with women. Maura rehashed the events of the night before. "It was very intense," she said as she ran her finger along the rim of a bread plate. "Dean was beside himself, and then Stephanie—"

"I don't mean to interrupt, but is that your cell phone?"

"Oh, I was so caught up in my story, I didn't notice." Maura pulled her cell phone from her backpack as the server delivered their meals.

"Hi, Steph, what's up?"

"I won't keep you," Stephanie said. "I'm just calling to see if Dean and I can come over tomorrow. We'd like to talk a little more."

"Of course, what time?"

"Two?"

"Perfect, I'll see you tomorrow."

Maura placed her phone back in her backpack. Once again, an appetizing meal sat in front of her, but her appetite was gone.

* * * * * * * * * * * * * *

Dean and Stephanie sank into the plump beige-and-white-striped cushions of the brown wicker sofa.

"This looks nice, Mom," said Dean as he eyed the screened porch and backyard.

"Thanks, I've been working out here the past few days." A glimpse of the past flashed through her mind: She and Paul used to drink their morning coffee on the porch during the warm weather months. They would sit on the wicker rocking chairs, reading the newspaper, sharing articles, and refilling coffee cups until they were ready to start the day. They would eat on the outdoor table, situated on the other side of the porch, across from the sitting area. They even hooked up a television, essentially turning the porch into a summer family room.

"So, what's going on?" Maura said as Dean and Stephanie helped themselves to the homemade sweet tea and gingersnaps she'd set out.

"Well," Stephanie said, "after we left your house last night, we ended up back at mine for a drink. One thing led to another, and we started talking about the DNA test again. We aren't quite sure when or how to break the news to the kids, and we wanted to hear your thoughts."

"Oh, thank you for including me. Actually, I've been thinking about that too." She sipped her tea. "The results should be delivered soon, and I know Sally is counting the days, but until you decide if you want to connect with Anna, I think we should hold off sharing the information. We can just say that the lab has a backlog. But the bigger issue is probably deciding how you want to move forward in terms of contacting Anna or not."

"Do you have to call her by her name?" Dean said with a grimace.

"She is a real person, Dean," Maura said sharply, "and her name is Anna." She took a calming breath. "How would you both feel about speaking with my counselor on Wednesday? I met with her last week, and she may be able to help you sort out what to do next."

Stephanie looked at Dean. "I'm game. We might be in over our heads here. You in?"

Dean rolled his eyes. "All right, if it will help life to return to some degree of normality."

Maura jumped up from her seat and squeezed herself in between Dean and Stephanie, wrapping an arm around each. "We'll get through this. Trust me. It's just a matter of time."

CHAPTER 11

"Your time is limited, so don't waste it living someone else's life."

— Steve Jobs

Maura pulled her bathing cap snugly over her ears, pressed on her goggles, and slid into the pool. After an hour of drills and an array of swim sets, she cooled down and headed to the locker room. "Hey, Lonnie, I didn't expect to see you here this late in the morning."

"I don't have to be in the office until this afternoon, so I thought I'd get a little more workout in."

"You really are serious this time," Maura said as Lonnie headed for the showers. "Just be careful you don't burn out."

Maura lagged behind, gathering her toiletries before she started toward the shower area. She spied Lonnie's robe hanging on a hook and selected the stall next to hers. As she pulled back the shower curtain, a loud thud emanated from

Lonnie's stall.

"Lonnie!" she screamed, momentarily flashing back to the last time she'd heard someone thud to the ground. She drew back the curtain to reveal Lonnie slumped in the corner, her head between her knees.

"I'm okay," Lonnie said weakly. "I felt faint, and then down I went. I don't think I hurt anything."

"Let me help you up." Maura grabbed Lonnie's robe and draped it over her shoulders. She shimmied into the stall, slid her forearms under Lonnie's armpits, and hoisted her up. Then she guided her to a bench. "Sit here. Are you still light-headed?"

"I'm fine. I guess I've been pushing too hard, cutting back on calories and upping the workouts. My trainer told me to slow down and to make a point of hydrating, but I didn't listen."

"Promise me you will go to see your doctor today and tell her what happened."

"I promise." Lonnie rambled on in apology for several more minutes.

"Lonnie, stop. I'm just glad I was here. Are you sure you're okay?"

"I am. Go ahead and shower. I'll see you by the lockers."

* * * * * * * * * * * * * *

Maura set her cell on the counter and plugged it into the charger. She barely released her grasp before the familiar ringtone sounded. Her heart skipped a beat when she saw Lonnie's name appear on the screen. "Hi, how are you? Is everything okay?"

"Hi, and yes, I saw my doctor. Everything checked out fine."

"That's such good news."

"I'm so embarrassed by this morning. I should never have allowed that to happen."

"There's no need to be embarrassed. It was an accident."

"One I could have avoided! Anyway, I was wondering if you're free tonight. I want to thank you for your help. You could come over here, and I'll show you my place. And for a change, *I'll* make dinner."

"I would love that."

"Great. And by the way, can we keep this morning's events between us?"

* * * * * * * * * * * * *

Two hours later Maura rang the bell at Lonnie's townhouse.

Lonnie opened the front door, and the smiley faces sprinkled across her apron matched her own. "Welcome," she said, gesturing for Maura to enter.

"These are for you," Maura said, handing over a small bouquet of multicolored tulips. "You gave me quite a scare this morning."

"I can only imagine," said Lonnie, leading Maura into her great room. "How did you know tulips are my favorite?"

"Lucky guess." Maura glanced around, struck by the mid-century modern style, the clean lines, and the muted color. Sharp and cool, much like Lonnie.

"Can I get you a glass of wine?" Lonnie asked as she approached a wine bucket atop her sleek white marble island.

"Please. And Lonnie, this place is gorgeous!"

"Why, thank you. I'm so glad you're here." She poured and delivered the wine. "Come, sit down."

Maura melted into the buttery upholstery of the light-gray leather sectional and sighed. "This is so comfortable. I feel so relaxed."

"Good. I'm sure I pushed your stress meter to the limit this morning."

"Oh, Lonnie, it's not like you planned it."

Lonnie swiped a celery stick through the bowl of hummus on the acrylic coffee table. "I've been doing a lot of soul-searching." She paused. "I've finally accepted the fact that I use food to gain a sense of control. If I feel vulnerable or inadequate, I stuff those feelings down with food. And in my profession, there is no room for insecurity."

"I'm sure that's true."

"I'm ready to finally get my eating habits under control, but I may need a little more support to stay on track. I don't want to substitute working out for eating, so I reached out to Josie for some counselor recommendations."

"Good for you. I love the person she recommended to me. Speaking of which, my kids have agreed to go to a group session with me tomorrow. I just hope they'll find some clarity." Not wanting to perseverate on her own insecurities, she changed the subject. "By the way, what are you making for dinner? It smells amazing."

Lonnie stood up and grinned. "Come on, I'll show you."

Maura linked her arm through Lonnie's as they made their way into the kitchen, ready to bond once more over good food.

CHAPTER 12

They always say time changes things, but you actually have to change them yourself.

— Andy Warhol

It wasn't a hard choice to make. It was Wednesday morning, and Maura could either pedal a stationary bike in a dark, cramped spin studio, or she could take Amelia out for a ride. She chose Amelia, named after Amelia Earhart.

While Paul had always swooned over his shiny red corvette, Maura's "other love" was Amelia, a red 2018 Cannondale road bike. It was lightweight, and it fit her like a glove. When she descended a hill with her hands on the drops—the curved downward portion of the handlebars—it placed her in an aerodynamic position that allowed her to feel like a pilot flying a bright-red Lockheed.

She had been an avid rider for years, buying her first bike when the kids were in middle school. Twice a week, after seeing them off to school, she would ride with a local all-female triathlon club. But one woman had moved away, another had crashed and given up riding, and a third had taken a job requiring travel, so the group had dissolved. Maura, however, had continued to ride solo.

She straddled the top tube of her bike and placed the cleat of her left cycling shoe into the pedal clip. Then she pulled the pedal up until her thigh and shin created a ninety-degree angle. Finally, she pushed down and mounted the seat. Gliding down the driveway, she clipped her right foot in and completed the first pedal stroke of the season.

She giggled aloud. "It's like riding a bike!"

Taking her bike for the season-opening ride felt like being reacquainted with an old friend. She turned out of her neighborhood into the wind and rode a fifteen-mile loop, consisting of mostly flat roads with a few rolling hills. An hour later, she cruised back onto her driveway and pressed a button on the matchbook-sized computer attached to her handlebars to check average speed. *Not bad for the first ride of the season.* It wasn't until she scrolled through the screen and saw the time that her stomach lurched. In two hours, she was meeting Dean and Stephanie at Lydia's counseling center.

* * * * * * * * * * * * *

Maura leaned against her car and watched as Stephanie's SUV sped up the gravel driveway, kicking up stones before jerking to a halt.

"I thought we were going to be late," huffed Stephanie as

she jumped from the driver's seat. "Dean was dragging his feet."

Dean responded with a shrug of his shoulders and a smirk.

"I'm just glad you're here," Maura said. "Follow me."

"You must be Dean," said Lydia as she greeted them in the parlor. "And you must be Stephanie." She shook their hands. "It's so nice to meet you both. And I want you to know that I'm sorry for the loss of your father."

"Thank you," they said in unison before getting comfortable on the love seat across from Maura's chair.

Lydia positioned herself on a wing chair as well.

"Dean, Stephanie, your mother shared with me that you are looking for some clarity. Can you elaborate?"

"Yes," Stephanie quickly responded. "Our father never told us about our half-sibling, and now we don't know what to do with that information."

"I have an activity that may help you sort through your feelings."

She directed their attention to a large whiteboard on an easel near the fireplace. The word "DAD" was centered on the top. Below that were two columns marked "BEFORE" and "AFTER." Lydia instructed Dean and Stephanie to each pick up a sticky pad and marker from the coffee table.

"I'd like you to think back to when you were children, and on a sticky note, I want you to write one word that described your father. Then attach it to the board under the BEFORE heading." It took only a moment for them to complete the task.

"Stephanie, I see you wrote the word 'Protector,'" said Lydia. "Can you explain?"

"Well, when I was little, Dad made me feel safe." Her dimples became pronounced. "He kept the monsters under my bed at bay."

"Dean, can you explain your word?"

"Hero," he said, his tone measured, but the rigid cords in his neck hinted at something else. "That says it all. He was my coach, my role model. I thought he could do anything."

Next, Lydia directed them to write words that described how they viewed their father once they became adults, and to place them in the BEFORE column.

Maura listened as they explained their word choices, and in the process, they painted a picture of a kind, supportive, and wise man.

"So," said Lydia, "can we agree that the two of you loved and admired your father very much?"

They both nodded.

Lydia instructed them to write down words describing their father after they'd learned he had another child, and to put them in the AFTER column.

"Stephanie, can you tell me about one of the words you've written?"

"Sure. I chose 'Disconnected' because I feel like Dad was living in denial of the fact that he had a third child. He must not have wanted to deal with it, so he pretended it didn't happen."

"How do you feel about that?" asked Lydia.

"It makes me feel awful for his other daughter. I can't imagine how she must have felt when she realized her father had abandoned her."

"I wrote 'Fraud,'" Dean sputtered. "What kind of man abandons his child and then presents himself as Father of the Year? I grew up thinking he was a superhero. Then as an adult, he became my best friend and mentor. I feel like he sold us a lie!" He shot up out of his seat. "I'm sorry, Mom, I can't do this. It makes my blood boil. Lydia, I'm done for today." He turned and made a beeline for the door.

"Dean, please!" cried Maura, rising from her chair. "Please come back. It will help to talk about it."

"Talking doesn't change the truth!" he called back as he stormed outside.

"Dean, wait up!" shouted Stephanie before turning to her mother. "I'm sorry, I've got to follow him." A moment later, she was gone.

Maura dropped back into her chair. "There you have it. What am I supposed to do?"

"It's like I said before," Lydia said. "This is going to take time. You can't fix this for them; they have to reconcile this in their own way. They obviously have a strong bond, and they'll continue to talk it out." Lydia poured them each a glass of water before continuing. "In terms of forging a relationship with their half-sister, they will each have to decide how to move forward, either together or alone. They're adults. This isn't your issue; your role is to support their decision."

"Supporting them, that's my M.O." Maura sipped her water, then lowered her voice to a confessional whisper. "I feel guilty for saying this, but a piece of me feels like I've spent my life taking a back seat to everyone else, picking up the pieces and gluing them back together. I've been a cheerleader and a silent partner." Her voice caught in her throat.

"Well, your husband passed away, and your children are grown. Next week, let's talk about how you'll define yourself in the next chapter of your life."

* * * * * * * * * * * * *

Maura woke parched, a symptom she attributed to involuntary mouth breathing, not the snoring that Paul used to suggest. Once again, after her counseling session, Maura had returned home and crashed. She prided herself on being punctual, but by the time she walked into Al Dente, where she was meeting the girls for dinner, she was fifteen minutes late. She scanned the cavernous space and spied Josie, Kara, and Lonnie at a large round table in the center of the crowded room. She hurried over. "Sorry I'm late. I was so wiped out after counseling that I fell asleep again." She slid into a seat next to Kara.

"That's okay," Kara said. "Nicole is showing a house and running late too."

"We went ahead and ordered these," said Josie, pointing to two bottles of wine. "Red or white?"

"White would be great."

"So, how did it go?"

"Well, the short story is that when things got uncomfortable, Dean stormed out and Stephanie followed. I just keep reminding myself that they have to work through this, and it will take time."

"Hi, everyone!" said Nicole, approaching the table breathlessly. "Can someone please pour me a glass of wine? I don't even care which kind."

Josie filled her glass with deep-red Chianti.

"What a nightmare that was!" Nicole exclaimed after gulping her drink. "I was showing a house to a couple with four young kids. The husband wanted to take a look at the basement, and the wife decided to tag along, so we left the kids upstairs. When we came back up, two of the kids had helped themselves to a snack, and the others were trying to corner the family cat!"

"Oh no!" said Maura as the rest of the women chuckled.

"That's not the worst part," Nicole said. "I have three more homes to show them tomorrow. All I can say is I'd better get a big commission out of this."

"Speaking of houses," Kara said, "Jack and I are thinking of downsizing."

"Really?" Maura said. "I thought you loved your house."

"We do, but a smaller house, or even a large townhouse, might be more practical. We're tired of all the effort, not to mention the money, that it costs to keep things going. And Trisha's been out of the house for years, so it might be time for a change."

"Let me know when you're ready," said Nicole. "If you'd like, I'd be happy to help."

"Sounds like you're turning a page," Maura said, feeling a strange mix of optimism and apprehension. But maybe Lydia had been right. Maybe it was time to think about the next chapter.

CHAPTER 13

"Let everything happen to you,
beauty and terror.
Just keep going. No feeling is final."

— Rainer Maria Rilke

Friday morning's class ended with a collective groan. Maura wiped the droplets of sweat from the wooden studio floor before entering the storage closet to return her equipment.

"Hey," called Eric, squeezing his lanky frame in beside Maura, "how are you making out?"

"I'm all right. Thanks for asking."

"Cool. I noticed how distracted you were last week." He ran his hand through his sweat-drenched sandy-colored hair. "I'm glad to see you're back on your game." His baby blues twinkled as he raised a clenched hand and tapped his knuckles against Maura's. "A bunch of us are going out Saturday night for Cinco de Mayo. You know the drill—tacos and tequila. We'll be at Salsa, seven-thirty, if you're free."

"I'll think about it," she said as she recalled the many fun times she and Paul had enjoyed with her workout crew. Unlike the ladies she'd befriended in the locker room, the folks she trained with had been socializing for years. "I'm not sure if I'm up for that yet," she continued, placing her medicine ball on the rack.

"I get it. Just wanted to throw out the invite. C'mon, I'll walk with you."

Maura smiled as she said goodbye to Eric and entered the locker room. At a youthful fifty-five, Eric was definitely still a "guy's guy." He loved playing and watching sports and could trash-talk with the best of them, but he was just as comfortable working out in a roomful of women and kibitzing after class. Maura often wondered why no one had snagged him yet.

"Happy Friday, girls," Maura said to Nicole and Lonnie near the hair-drying station.

"You've got that right," said Nicole. "By the way, I survived yesterday's showings, and they put an offer on a super-cute ranch."

"That's great," said Maura on her way to the showers.

"Hi, Maura," called Josie, wrapped in a towel. "I'm glad I ran into you. I'm going into New York City tomorrow to see the Joseph Turner exhibit. Want to join me?"

Maura didn't miss a beat. "I'd love to. I haven't been to the city or an art gallery in far too long."

"Great. Pick you up tomorrow at ten? We could grab lunch beforehand."

"Perfect. By the way, what museum are we going to?"

"The Frick. Have you been?"

"No."

"You're in for a treat. See you tomorrow."

* * * * * * * * * * * * *

After a quick breakfast, Maura jumped into her car and drove to the Galleria. She and Paul used to laugh about the fact that they felt like hillbillies, gawking at the sights and sounds when they made their yearly Christmastime trek to shop. Living in a small coastal town, they liked to support local businesses when they could, but they were always drawn to the sheer seasonal consumerism of the mall during the holidays. When the kids were little, she and Paul would divide and conquer; the boys would race the girls to see who could get their shopping done first, and the winners would choose a restaurant for an early dinner before going home.

She felt a familiar tightening in her chest, so she returned to her favorite mantra: *Breathe slow and deep, and the sadness will subside.*

* * * * * * * * * * * * *

Maura hung her new purchases in the closet. The lightweight black-and-white-checked slacks, crisp white blouse, and red cardigan were as classic as she was. She slipped her feet into the black leather loafers she'd bought that afternoon and went downstairs to prepare for the family's arrival.

Blip. Her stomach dropped when she saw an email from the DNA testing company on her phone. It was a short message: *Due to an increase in volume, we are currently two weeks behind schedule. We apologize for the delay and will send an update soon.*

Before she could exhale a sigh of relief, her phone sounded again. Her pulse quickened when she saw Dean was calling.

"Hi, Dean."

"Hi. I wanted to touch base before we come over tonight."

She felt her clenched jaw relax. "I'm glad you're coming."

"Listen, I apologize for my recent tantrums. I just get so crazy at the thought of Dad abandoning Anna. Anyway, I wanted you to know that I called Lydia."

"Oh!"

"I'm going to see her next week. By myself. Stephanie convinced me that it's in my best interest, and I agree. I can't keep flying off the handle. Lydia said she'll work with me on coping skills."

"Dean, I'm so proud of you."

"I just wanted to clear the air. I know this hasn't been easy for you, and I'm sorry if I've made things harder."

"I appreciate that. And don't worry, we'll get through this." She cleared her throat in an attempt to maintain her composure.

"I know. I'll see you in a few."

Maura placed her phone back on the counter and savored the moment. Between the delay in DNA results and Dean's call, she felt more hopeful than she had since this whole ordeal began.

CHAPTER 14

"We're so busy watching out for what's just ahead of us that we don't take time to enjoy where we are."

– Bill Watterson

"I know Paris in the spring is iconic," said Maura, "but Josie, it can't be any more beautiful than this."

A slight breeze drifted through the open-air deck at The Loeb Boathouse, a landmark on the lake in Central Park. They were seated next to a black wrought-iron rail—prime real estate in the restaurant, which was popular with tourists and locals alike. Rowboats filled with couples young and old glided through the glassy water that lapped the base of the deck. It was spring, and as the cliché went, *love was in the air.*

"I hope I'm not being too bold," said Maura, "but you've never mentioned dating. Do you have someone special?"

Josie drew her hand to her heart. "I did. Her name was

Diane." She lowered her hand, pinched the stem of her glass, and took a sip of wine. "She died of cancer ten years ago. It was right before I joined The Coastal Club."

Maura scooted forward in her seat and angled her body closer to the table.

"As a matter of fact," Josie continued, "I was having a hard time dealing with grief. It was suggested daily exercise might be helpful. That's when I joined The Club. It gave me a reason to get out of bed. Then I met you and the others. But it just never felt like the right time to share my story, and as time went by, it never came up."

"I'm so sorry! Tell me about her."

Josie glanced into the distance with an adoring gaze. "Diane loved life and lived it to the fullest. To say she was the life of the party was an understatement. She was adventurous, funny, charismatic, and compassionate." Josie raised her head slightly, tilting her chin upward. "We were together for fifteen years when she was diagnosed with breast cancer." She paused for another mouthful of wine. "She fought such a hard fight, but even her strong will couldn't beat it. She was the love of my life." She rolled the stem of her wine glass between her hands without seeming to realize she was doing it. "After her, no one else can compare. It's enough for me that I got to experience life with her for as long as I did. I have no regrets."

For the remainder of the meal, Josie shared anecdotes from her time with Diane. Some were amusing, some were touching, and some were outrageous. When the waiter brought the check, Josie smiled. "Thank you for asking, Maura. It felt good to talk about her. Sharing those memories keeps her close."

"Thank you for sharing those stories with me. I'm sorry I

never got to know Diane; she sounds like a very special person. And thank you for inviting me to the art exhibit. I once saw an intriguing movie about Joseph Turner, and I can't believe I'm about to see his paintings."

It was a short walk to The Frick Collection, one of the less famous museums in New York City. Of modest size, it was housed in a grand old estate on Fifth Avenue that had once been home to Henry Clay Frick, a Pittsburgh industrialist.

They entered the museum and headed straight for the Turner exhibit. It was everything they hoped it would be. His famous seascapes were both ominous and energized.

After passing through the exhibit, they meandered about, taking in the paintings, sculptures, and porcelain.

"Can you imagine what it would have been like to live in this grandeur?" said Josie.

"I think I could have handled it."

By the time Maura returned home, the setting sun had painted the clouds with brilliant reds and golden-yellow hues. The crowd from the gym would be meeting to celebrate Cinco de Mayo, and the thought of seeing Eric and the gang was tempting, but trapezing around the city had taken its toll. She settled for a quiet night at home.

* * * * * * * * * * * * *

On Monday, Maura and the others survived another Extreme Boot Camp and were rehashing it outside the studio door.

"I couldn't have done one more sprint," said Maura.

"The burpees had me imagining my epitaph. If I had to do one more, I would have passed out," added Beth, who, regardless of complaining, craved intense workouts like a racer craves speed.

"Hey, Maura," called Eric as he approached. "You missed a good time on Saturday night."

"Too good of a time," said Beth as she slapped the palm of her hand against her forehead. "I paid for it yesterday."

Maura giggled. "I ended up going into the city for the day, and once I got home, I was too exhausted to do anything."

"Next time, no excuses," said Eric before winking. "See you two tomorrow," he called over his shoulder.

Maura couldn't help but grin.

In the locker room, she almost collided with Lonnie, whose ragged gym bag created a beautiful contrast with her tailored navy-blue suit and nude patent leather heels.

"Court?" asked Maura.

"How did you know?" Lonnie said sarcastically. "But this is a great suit, isn't it? I went shopping with Nicole on Saturday."

"Well, good luck today," said Maura, holding up crossed fingers.

"It ain't about luck," said Lonnie, her right eyebrow arching.

* * * * * * * * * * * * *

The hours slipped away as Maura checked items off the list that Dean helped her create weeks ago. For the first time in years, she had a credit card in her own name, and the car and house titles had been transferred to her as well. As the list dwindled, she vacillated from being overwhelmed to feeling emboldened.

The sun had sunk by the time she closed her laptop. She

grabbed a sweater and a half-read romance novel. The latter would offer a pleasant escape. Similar to exercising, reading somehow suspended time for her. Then she searched for her glasses, bothered by the fact that she never needed them before but now couldn't read a thing without them. The readers were right where she'd left them, on the kitchen counter next to her cell. She slid them on and checked the phone to reveal a missed call from Stephanie.

"Sorry I missed your call," Maura said upon reaching Stephanie.

"I wanted to talk to you about something."

The butterflies in Maura's stomach woke up. "I'm all ears."

"Dean and I would like your help with something."

"Anything," replied Maura.

Stephanie hesitated before speaking again. "Can you tell the kids about Anna? We feel like the news will make more sense if it comes from you."

Like a dying plant given fresh water, Maura felt her anger at Paul taking root again. She took her time before responding and wandered out to the screened porch where she sunk into one of the wicker rockers. "I thought you were going to wait a while before mentioning Anna to them."

"That was our initial thought, but we're afraid they might overhear one of us talking. We think the best thing to do is to be upfront. No secrets. Secrets are what got us into this dilemma."

Maura couldn't dispute that. "You're right, of course. I'll talk with them this Friday night."

"Thanks, Mom. I've got to go; I have to pick Sally up from softball practice."

"Give her a hug for me."

Maura placed her phone down. *How will this mess turn out?*

She picked up her book and peered at the lovey-dovey couple on the cover. *At least this story will end happily.* She nestled into the chair, removed her bookmark, and for the next hour, lost herself in someone else's drama.

* * * * * * * * * * * * *

Maura didn't count the laps she swam. She had no sense of how long she had been propelling her body from one end of the pool to the other. Instead, she focused on how she would explain the existence of Anna to her grandchildren. By the time she entered the locker room, it was deserted. She dressed quickly, dried her hair, and headed to the parking lot.

As she clicked her seatbelt, a growl followed by a gurgle startled her, but it was her own stomach. She steered her car toward the coffee shop in town. With a morning glory muffin and small coffee in hand, she planted herself at the counter that ran along the front window of the shop—a perfect spot to people-watch.

"Is this seat taken?"

Maura turned and was surprised to see Eric, whose bright smile stretched cheek to cheek. In his hands, he held a coffee and an onion bagel.

"Good morning," she said, gesturing to the empty stool next to hers. "And no, I was saving it just for you," she teased.

Eric settled in next to Maura. "I've got an idea. Let's play Faces and Places, a game I made up. You pick out a person walking by and make up a story about them. See that kid wearing the Hurley cap? He's on his way to the beach where he's meeting his best friend's girl. Little does he know that his ex-best friend is meeting him instead and is gonna beat the crap out of him!"

Maura flinched. "Ouch! See that woman across the street with a yellow jacket and short silver hair? She's on her way home from an overnight at her young lover's house. They've been carrying on a clandestine relationship for six months. She's afraid her children will disapprove."

Eric glanced at the older woman and gave a thumbs-up. "You go, girl!" He paused, scanning the passersby. "Ah, see that woman in the navy skirt and sensible shoes? She dreamt of going to Hollywood and becoming a movie star, but her roommate stole her plane ticket before skipping out on the lease, and she's been stuck working at the bank ever since."

"So sad," said Maura. "Look at them." She pointed to a couple. The man was frowning and was very animated as he spoke. The woman walked a half-step behind, her arms folded tightly across her chest. "They don't know it, but yesterday they bought a winning lottery ticket. By this time tomorrow, they will be rich beyond their wildest dreams. The only problem is, they're in the process of breaking up at this very moment!"

"Oh boy. Who's holding the winning ticket?"

"Exactly!"

After several rounds, Eric looked at his watch. "Oh man, I'm so glad I ran into you, and I hate to run, but I don't want to be blamed for world travel coming to a halt." He jumped up, gave Maura a quick kiss on the cheek, and hurried out to open his travel agency.

Maura leaned back in her stool and sipped her coffee as she tried to imagine the rest of Eric's day.

CHAPTER 15

"The way we spend our time defines who we are."

— Johnathan Estrin

On Wednesday, Maura awoke to the rumble of a garbage truck snaking its way down her street. The sun was shining brightly. The bedroom curtains billowed softly in the breeze. She checked the bedside clock and decided to forgo her workout. *There's always tomorrow,* she thought, but was immediately struck by another thought: *unless there isn't.* She reached for her phone and sent a group text to the supper club: *Sorry I missed you this morning. Slept in. See you tonight at 6:30.*

* * * * * * * * * * * * *

Maura entered Lydia's now-familiar parlor, found her place on the loveseat, and wondered what the therapist had in store for her today.

Lydia explained that although she wanted to focus on Maura's next chapter, she needed Maura to visit the past to see how far she'd strayed from her original path.

"Maura, you are going to do an activity similar to what I had Dean and Stephanie do last week. As you can see, I've created another chart on the whiteboard, this time labeled THEN and NOW." She gestured toward the stack of sticky notes resting on the coffee table. "I want you to write a word on three of these sticky notes describing what you wanted at the start of your marriage. Then attach them to the board."

Maura finished the task in an instant.

"I see you have written 'Children.'"

"Yes," said Maura. "Having no siblings, Paul and I dreamed of having a large family."

"What happened? Did you have trouble conceiving?"

"Quite the contrary. Dean and Stephanie were conceived right on schedule."

"Was it a financial issue?"

"No, and it wasn't a matter of timing either." She sighed and picked at the nail of her middle finger, a habit she'd been trying to break since childhood. "I've never told this to anyone, but I made a conscious decision not to have any more children. Paul never knew."

Lydia shifted forward but stayed quiet.

"Do you remember I told you how Paul wept when he held Dean?"

"Yes."

"And that I felt he was crying for his firstborn, Anna?"

"Mm-hmm," said Lydia, cocking her head.

"What I didn't tell you was that the moment he held

Stephanie for the first time, I was the one who sobbed."

"Why was that?"

"I saw Paul holding our little girl, and it occurred to me that this was not the first time he'd held a newborn daughter. I couldn't reconcile the fact that the kind of man who would turn his back on his own child was now the father of my children."

Maura felt disembodied from her voice. She knew she was the one talking, but to hear the words spoken aloud seemed surreal. She picked at the fingernail she'd been working on until a sliver tore free. She rolled it absentmindedly between her thumb and index finger.

"I remember feeling overwhelmed with despair. How could I have willingly created life with a man who could turn his back on his own blood?" Tears pooled in her eyes. "That's when I knew I would not bear any more of his children."

Her cheeks began to tingle, and her palms felt clammy. She swallowed hard to dissolve the lump in her throat. *I can't believe I'm going to tell someone this.*

"I secretly went on birth control pills and led him to believe that two children were all I could handle." She grabbed a tissue and dabbed her eyes.

"How does that decision make you feel?"

"For a long time, I was angry and depressed. I felt like he had taken my dream from me; I felt like I had made a mistake marrying him." Pressing her palms together, she slid her hands between her thighs as she rocked forward and back, ever so slightly. For several moments, the room was draped in silence. "What must you think of me?"

Lydia sat taller, pulling back her shoulders. "I think at that time and place, you made the best decision you could."

What Maura heard was, *Who would ever do a thing like that?* She cringed.

"Maura, I need you to hear me. You've punished yourself long enough. You can't undo the past. All you can do is accept the present and look to the future." She redirected Maura to the whiteboard. "I see you've written the word 'Work.' Can we talk about that?"

Maura grinned. "I wanted to be a teacher from the time I was a little girl. I worked a few years before starting a family, but when Paul suggested I stay at home with the children, I agreed. I had pushed the idea that two children were all I could handle. We could afford it, and with Paul's work and travel schedule, it made sense."

"Any regrets?"

"Initially, of course. I felt that once again I was giving up on my dream, but I decided early on not to be bitter about compromising my happiness when I chose to have only two children and give up my career. I won't say those feelings didn't bubble up from time to time; however, I was committed to staying in my marriage and raising my kids with their father." She paused. "To be honest, sometimes I'm envious of my friend Kara. She raised a family and taught at the same time. It hasn't always been easy for her, but she takes such pride in what she does."

Maura filled her glass. Her mouth was dry, and the water tasted cool and refreshing.

"I've been a volunteer reader at the elementary school," she continued, "ever since Dean and Stephanie attended, and I get a lot of satisfaction out of that. I mean, I know it's not the same as teaching, but it is rewarding." She leaned back and crossed her arms.

Lydia glanced at the whiteboard once more. “The last word on the board is ‘Adventure.’”

Maura’s hands dropped to her lap as she sat up. “I always wanted to travel. I read a lot, and there are so many places I visited in stories that I would love to have visited in person. But between Paul’s work schedule and the kids’ activities, it just wasn’t in the cards.”

“Tell me how you feel about that.”

Maura rubbed her right arm. “I’m disappointed. Paul and I planned to travel once he retired, and now that’s not going to happen.” She tilted her head back. “I certainly don’t want to gallivant all over the world by myself.”

“What I see is someone who gave up on her dreams in order to meet the needs of everyone else. How could you not feel angry or resentful?”

“It’s a choice I made.” Maura heard the pitch of her voice rising, her intensity growing. “I grew up without a father. After a dysfunctional marriage, my parents divorced. I know what it’s like to be raised by a struggling single mother, and I didn’t want that for my children.” Maura breathed deeply, her eyes looking inward. “You might say I sold my soul to the devil, but I was able to raise my children with a father. I was able to raise them in a beautiful home. They had a happy childhood. It was worth the price.”

“What was the price?”

Maura peered into Lydia’s eyes, her face expressionless. “I faked it.” She began to play with the drawstring on the waistband of her pants, coiling it around her index finger. “I pretended it was enough for me. Don’t get me wrong; there were good times, and Paul wasn’t loathsome. We fell into a pleasant existence. We weren’t especially passionate, but it worked. We were good partners." She shrugged. "So I didn't have all my needs met. Who does?"

"We get what we believe we deserve."

Maura's head tilted right, her eyes questioning, like a puppy looking for direction from her owner.

Lydia took her cue and elaborated. "We all set a bar for ourselves. The level of that bar depends on our self-worth. The more insecure we are, the lower we set the bar. Conversely, the more confident we are, the higher we set the bar."

Maura shifted in her seat, crossed her right leg over her left, and knitted her fingers together. She wasn't aware of her clenched teeth until she opened her mouth to respond. "If that's the case, the question becomes, how do I build self-confidence?"

"Well, the first step is to make yourself a priority, an idea I believe you've grappled with for a long time." She redirected Maura to the sticky notes. "Let's move ahead and think about the present. I want you to write words that describe you at this moment."

When the words were in place on the board, Lydia began again. "I see the word 'Responsible.' Tell me about that."

"I took care of Paul and the children's needs. I paid the bills and made sure deadlines for the kids were met. Now that I have grandchildren, I chip in whenever needed."

"Explain 'Supportive.'"

"I supported Paul by handling our children and household issues so that he could focus on work. I supported the children by enabling them to pursue their interests and goals, and I cheer on the grandkids now."

Lydia read the final phrase. "Problem Solver."

"When Paul had a problem at work, I was his sounding

board. The children came to me for advice—and still do. For example, they just asked *me* to explain Anna to the grandchildren. And if the grandkids are in a pickle, I help them out when I can."

Lydia returned to the board and wrote three words of her own: "husband," "children," and "grandchildren."

Maura read the words aloud, her right foot twitching up and down. Her eyes darted back and forth from the whiteboard to Lydia. "I see what you're doing. You're saying that I'm defining myself through them and their needs."

"You catch on quickly."

"I've been a stay-at-home mom for thirty-plus years!" shrieked Maura, the venom in her voice startling her. "I apologize for my tone, Lydia, but really, what do you expect?"

"This isn't about my expectations, Maura. It's about your perceptions."

Lydia's steady voice and relaxed face annoyed Maura.

"I need a moment." Maura leaned her head back and stared at the ceiling before dropping her chin to her chest. *You're not going to make any progress if you don't trust her and this process. You've already spilled the beans about the birth control pills; there's no going back now!*

Maura shook her head slowly. "All right, I'm ready to continue."

"Think back to the young woman you were just prior to getting married. Give me a word to describe her."

"Wow, I haven't thought about her in a long time." She closed her eyes and ran her fingers back and forth across her forehead as if manually reviving the woman she once was. After a long while, she rested her hands in her lap, opened her eyes, and sighed. "Excited," she said flatly, trying to put up a wall to protect herself from the overwhelming sadness lurking just beneath the surface.

"About what?" asked Lydia, writing the word down.

"About all that life had to offer. I assumed I could have it all. I was in love with a man who was everything I'd hoped for. He was kind, stable, and goal-driven. I was about to begin the career of my dreams. Life was good."

"Give me another word."

Maura unearthed another buried descriptor of her younger self. "'Engaged,'" she said in a tone just louder than a whisper.

"Explain."

"I was part of something bigger than me. I was focused on my job. I was making a difference." For the second time today, emotion threatened to overwhelm her. She bit her lip to stop it from quivering.

"And give me one more word."

Maura's voice cracked. "'Fearless.' I felt like anything was possible and that I could do whatever I put my mind to."

"Well," declared Lydia as she handed the tissue box to Maura. "That is the woman we're going to find again. That is the woman who will craft a plan for the future."

"Do you really think I can find her again?"

Lydia pressed her hands together as if in prayer and placed her chin on her fingertips. A smile formed on her lips as she stared into Maura's eyes. "I know you can find her again. You have many years ahead. The entire second half awaits—"

"Or at least the fourth quarter!"

Lydia giggled. "It's time for you to focus on yourself." She tapped an imaginary wristwatch. "The clock is ticking."

CHAPTER 16

"Our perception of time
is indeed our reality."

— Brigid Schulte

The Wednesday night supper club was in full swing with the ladies gathered in Maura's family room for drinks, snacks, and cherished, unhurried conversation before dinner. Maura scanned the room and smiled. *I'm so glad I didn't cancel after seeing Lydia this afternoon. This is exactly the therapy I need.*

"I've been waiting all day to fill you in on my husband Jack's dilemma," Kara said as she clasped her hands together. "His company is moving his division to Philadelphia, which means a seventy-mile commute each way. He's extremely frustrated because even though he'll be sixty-two in a few months, he didn't plan to retire, but now he doesn't think it's worthwhile to stay." She sipped her wine. "The thought of taking on a commute like that at this point, without any added financial compensation, does not appeal to him at all. And to make matters worse, it's common knowledge that the company will be happy to replace him with someone younger, at a lower salary." She got up to refill her snack plate. "I feel awful for him. This getting-older thing really stinks."

"Plan for the future, girls," said Maura. "It has a way of sneaking up on you."

Back in her seat with a full plate on her lap, Kara continued. "As you know, we've been considering downsizing, and this has confirmed that it's time." She turned to Nicole. "If it's okay with you, I'll call tomorrow. Maybe we can schedule some time to talk."

"Of course."

"I wonder if the perception of getting pushed out at the end of a career is a recent phenomenon or if it's always existed," said Josie.

"It certainly seems to be a reality," Maura said. "It happened several times at Paul's company."

"I even see it at school," added Kara. "Veteran teachers feel discounted. There's an 'in with the new, out with the old' culture. It ends up driving seasoned teachers out of the profession." She winked at Maura. "But they can't get rid of me that easily."

"While we're on the topic of careers," Lonnie said, glancing at Maura, "are you going to tell us why you never pursued some kind of culinary work?"

"It's funny you ask. Paul and I toyed with the idea of writing a family cookbook so we could share our recipes with the kids, but we never got around to it. For me, after Dean and Stephanie were born, raising them became my job, but in my session today, Lydia said it's time for me to quote-unquote define myself. Who knows? Maybe cooking will be a direction I'll take."

"I know what you can do!" said Nicole. "Make healthy meals to go. Instead of filling half-trays and freezing them, you can make single-meal options. The meals would be fresh, and you could change the menu daily. Customers could purchase them and pop them in the microwave for a quick, healthy meal."

"That's a great idea," said Lonnie. "I know I would love a healthy fast-food alternative, and I'm sure other people would too!"

"That's certainly worth giving thought to," said Maura. "Though it sounds financially and logistically overwhelming."

"All this talk about food is making me hungry," said Nicole. "Let's eat!"

As usual, Maura had pulled out an array of entree choices from her freezer stock. The spicy chickpea curry and rice with sweet roasted carrots filled the room with a musky bouquet. Sticky barbecue chicken thighs glistened in their tin next to a stack of crispy vegetable fritters, with an irresistible side bowl of homemade chunky applesauce. Juicy baked ham, tender roasted butternut squash, and tangy coleslaw made it impossible to fill a plate from just one tin.

Preparing dishes for these Wednesday night dinners had helped fill Maura's otherwise lonely hours. She'd always found cooking to be a creative outlet, but now it also served as a way to fill time. Prior to Paul's death, she'd scheduled her time around his itinerary. Now she had all the time in the world and found comfort in preparing delectable delights for supper club. She enjoyed every step, from creating the menus, to preparing the meals, to serving it all at just the right temperature.

"As usual, everything is delicious," said Josie, who'd taken a small sample of each dish. "I think Nicole might be onto something."

"If you ever want to do it, I can find you commercial kitchen space," said Nicole.

"I can help with any legal issues," added Lonnie.

"And Josie and I can taste-test!" said Kara.

"Well, thank you, all. I will keep it in mind," said Maura.

It was nearly ten o'clock before Maura was ready to end the day. She snuggled under the covers, closed her eyes, and imagined herself in the throes of commercialism:

She is in a small building located in the center of town. It's a bright, cheery space with two buffet-style counters, one for hot food, one for cold.

Customers fill containers and bring them to the service counter, where Maura chats with them as she weighs their selections and charges by the ounce.

In the evenings, she's busy in the kitchen preparing the next day's meals.

Her dreams that night remained culinary and heavenly scented.

Beep-beep-beep… As she reached over to turn off the alarm, last night's conversation came back to her. *What do I know about running my own business? Nothing! But I have to figure out the next chapter. I guess time will tell.*

* * * * * * * * * * * * * *

Maura rolled her eyes and pulled to the back of the line of cars waiting for students at Jake and Sally's elementary school.

Friday afternoon already. Where did this day go? Time is supposed to fly as you get older, but this is ridiculous.

A buzzer signaled the end of the school day, and hordes of children spilled from the building. A group of girls exited, their heads together as they made their way past Maura's car. A single boy strolled along with his head down as he fidgeted with his phone. Then three younger girls passed by, holding hands and singing as they went. Finally, Sally appeared, smiling and waving at Maura.

"Hi, Gran," she shouted as she jumped in the back seat.

"Don't forget to buckle."

"I won't. I am so excited to help make pizzas tonight. I thought today would never end."

Sally yakked for the entire ride, providing a play-by-play of her day. Maura smiled to herself. Sally was so much like her mother when she was little.

When they arrived at the house, Maura put Sally to work. "After you wash your hands, your first job is to empty these." She pointed to an open bag of sliced pepperoni, a container of sun-dried tomatoes, a jar of black olives, a plastic container of ricotta cheese, and a small bag of spinach. Then she gestured to the other side of the island. "And put them in those bowls."

While Sally filled the bowls, Maura browned some ground sausage.

"That smells so good, Gran. I want to eat it right now!"

"I almost forgot! I made a snack for you."

Maura opened the fridge and pulled out a small plate of peanut-butter-filled celery dotted with dark raisins.

"Ants on a log! My favorite!"

"And here's a drink to wash it down." Maura placed an ice-cold glass of milk in front of Sally. "When you're done, I have another job for you."

"I'm here to help." Sally grinned, peanut butter dotting her fingers and outlining her mouth.

"I'll get you a napkin."

"That's okay, Gran." With a swirl of her rosy pink tongue, she cleaned her fingers and mouth.

After snack time, Maura supervised as Sally sliced peppers and grated fresh mozzarella cheese.

"Let me show you a trick," said Maura. "If you run an onion under cold water before slicing, it won't make your eyes tear, and if it starts to, just run it under cold water again."

Maura demonstrated before passing the onion to Sally.

"How do you know that trick? Did a magician teach you?"

"No," said Maura with a laugh. "My grandmother showed me when I used to help her in the kitchen. I was probably your age, but instead of helping to make pizza, we'd make stew. We would cut up chunks of meat and chop carrots, celery, and onions. It would cook all day and the house would smell wonderful."

"Can we make stew together one day, please, Gran?"

"I would love to," Maura said as she leaned over and kissed the top of Sally's head. "Okay, enough chitchat. Let's get back to work."

By the time the rest of the family arrived, Maura and Sally had rolled out individual-sized pizza dough for each of them. A pizza stone was heating in the oven, and an antipasto was sitting in the center of the table for munching.

As usual, there were numerous claims as to who made the best pizza. When the meal was finished, everyone worked together to clear the table, and Maura pulled out three boxes of Tartufo from the freezer. Paul had lovingly referred to the ice cream balls covered in chocolate as boccie balls. She'd picked them up at the Italian specialty shop earlier.

When everyone gathered around the table with dessert in front of them, Maura explained to the grandchildren that she had a story to tell them about their grandfather.

"What is it, Gran?" asked Sam. "Tell us!"

"You remember that Pop grew up in a small town, don't you?"

"I do," said Sam. "I remember the time we went there to visit one of his friends. We went to a house party. There were lots of people and food, and we played with a bunch of kids."

"Yes, that was Pop's friend Tommy. He was Pop's best friend growing up. But it's another friend I want to talk about. You see, back when Pop was in high school, he had a girlfriend named Lisa."

"She wasn't pretty or nice," said Sally. "That's why he married you, right?"

Maura smiled. "When Pop and Lisa were seniors in high school, they had a baby—a little girl they named Anna."

"Where is she now?" asked Sam.

Maura's eyes darted from Dean to Stephanie in an unspoken plea for help.

"Let Gran finish," said Dean. He smiled and nodded, signaling Maura to continue.

Maura took a deep breath, then exhaled slowly. "Where was I? I remember. It wasn't long after Anna was born that Pop went off to college. He was very busy with his studies and"—she stared down at her clasped hands before looking up and continuing—"getting an education was very important to Pop."

"I know he liked A's," said Jake. "That's why he always

gave us five dollars for each one we got on our report card."

"Yes, he did," Maura said, chuckling. "And don't worry, I'll continue the tradition. Anyway, Pop lived away at college, and Lisa eventually met someone else, whom she married. That man adopted Anna, and they became a family. I met Pop years later, in graduate school, and we made our family. I told your parents about Anna for the first time recently. She is their half-sister, which makes her your aunt."

For what seemed like an eternity, no one made a sound.

Suddenly Jake broke the silence. "Awesome! That means more cousins."

"Yeah, but where is she?" asked Sam for the second time.

"That's the thing, buddy," replied Dean. "We have to figure that out."

"How?"

"You leave that part up to me and Aunt Stephanie."

Sam, Jake, and Sally spent the remainder of the evening hypothesizing how many more cousins they might have, how old they might be, their genders, likes, and dislikes.

Finally, it was time to end the gathering. As they headed for the door, Dean and Stephanie lagged behind.

"Thanks, Mom," said Dean, hugging Maura.

Maura reached for Stephanie and pulled her into their embrace. "Everything's going to be fine. Just give it time."

If only I believed that myself.

CHAPTER 17

"Time flies when you're having fun."

— *Albert Einstein*

The mid-May race marked the unofficial start of summer in Maura's seaside town. A gaggle of runners swarmed the registration table eager to get their race bibs, but Maura knew she had plenty of time before the singing of the National Anthem would signal the start of the annual five-mile race.

With a final safety pin, she secured her race number to her T-shirt, then scanned the crowd. It didn't take long to spot several workout buddies warming up in the nearby meadow.

"Who's ready to race?" she called, jogging toward the group.

"Is that a challenge?" said Eric, one eyebrow arching significantly higher than the other. "Because I can't resist a challenge!"

Maura played along. "What's in it for the winner?"

Eric squinted and pursed his lips. It wasn't but a moment

before his eyes and grin both widened. "Loser buys the winner breakfast after Monday's workout."

"Count me in." She moved toward Eric, her arm extended. "Shake?"

Eric's arm shot forward. The challenge was on.

* * * * * * * * * * * * *

"I'll see you at the finish," taunted Eric as he sprinted away from Maura at the fourth-mile marker.

She did her best to catch him but couldn't match his long, effortless stride.

"I can't believe you beat me!" she gasped at the finish line as she tried to regain her breath.

"I take no prisoners," he said, handing her a bottle of water and a banana. "Come on, let's try to find the others."

They wove through the crowd, locating one person here and another two there until all had regrouped.

"Okay, everyone," said Beth. "Who's ready to get this party started? Let's make our way over to my house for the tenth annual race-day barbecue."

"Let's go!" they all shouted in unison.

* * * * * * * * * * * * *

Beth's husband, Jimmy—spatula in one hand, Bloody Mary in the other—was waiting on the back deck when they arrived. "Welcome!" he said. "It's almost noon. Who's up for a breakfast burger and a Bloody?"

Jimmy's breakfast burgers were legendary, each juicy burger topped with pepper jack cheese and a sunny-side-up egg.

Maura made a beeline for the makeshift Bloody Mary bar. Along with several pitchers of the crimson concoction was an assortment of garnishes. She picked up a cocktail skewer and pierced a shrimp, a pickled jalapeno, and a crisp piece of bacon. Drink in hand, she strolled over to the grill.

"Jimmy, you are a grill master," she said before pecking his cheek.

"Hey, Maura, I'm glad to see you. It seems so strange not to have Paul here. I really miss my wingman. How are you doing?"

"Overall, I'm good, but I've got to tell you, sometimes it's just so hard."

"You know we're here for you."

"I appreciate that," she said, wishing the tingle in her belly could be credited to her spicy drink rather than the recollection of Paul and Jimmy's special bond.

Over the years, Paul and Jimmy had become good friends. Neither of them had exercised at The Coastal Club; nor had they participated in any of the club-sponsored events, but they had attended every race, cheering on the rest of the gang from the sidelines, waiting at every finish line with a towel and a drink. They'd also competed to see who could get their companies to donate the most for club-related charities. Once, when the club sponsored a twenty-four-hour charity spin class, Paul and Jimmy had manned the snack station together throughout the night, while Maura and Beth took turns spinning. They'd been the talk of the event when they showed up wearing matching T-shirts proclaiming, I DON'T DO SPIN, I DO A SPINNER.

In an attempt to dodge the grief balling up inside her,

Maura drove the conversation in a different direction. "We all appreciate you and Beth hosting, and—"

"Jimbo, you need a hand?" asked Eric as he joined them at the grill.

"Perfect timing," Jimmy replied. "Can you grab the carton of eggs and the toasted English muffins from inside?"

"I'm on it!" He headed for the kitchen.

"He's a good guy," said Jimmy.

"Yeah," Maura said, "I love this entire group. We have had a lot of good times together." She looked at the crowd mingling below. Laughter rang out from the seating area under the pergola, while on the far side of the yard, a foursome played cornhole.

"Looks like today won't disappoint," said Jimmy.

By late afternoon, the party began to wind down.

"It's been a while since I've laughed this much," said Maura as she and Beth gathered up empty glasses and discarded snack plates.

"It's so good to see you having fun," said Beth. "I know it's been rough, and I can't begin to know what you've been going through, but I think the old Maura is making a comeback,"

Maura shrugged her shoulders. "Now, I just have to figure out what I'm coming back as."

* * * * * * * * * * * * * *

After the race and barbecue, Maura had decided not to set her alarm, allowing herself to sleep in on Mother's Day. When she did open her eyes, she stared at the ceiling and recalled past Mother's Day celebrations. Breakfast in bed was a given when the children were little. They always took such pride in serving her jelly toast and hot chocolate. And then there were the gifts. She still had the poem that Dean wrote for her when he was nine, and the framed picture taken at Stephanie's kindergarten Mother's Day Tea.

But ever since Sam was born, Dean had taken over hosting duties. And once Stephanie became a mom, Kyle had jumped in to help. Today would be no different.

"Good day, ladies," Sally said as she handed flower-speckled homemade menus to Maura, Maddie, and Stephanie at Dean's house. "Here is today's menu. Can I get you a glass of fresh orange juice? Sam squeezed the oranges himself."

Before they could answer, Jake arrived carrying a tray with three glasses of bright orange juice.

"Jake," cried Sally, "I was just taking the juice order."

"Good, here it is." A huge grin spread across his face.

"Mom, make him take them back into the kitchen," demanded an exasperated Sally.

"It's okay, Sally," Stephanie said. "We were all going to order a glass anyway." She opened the menu. "Explain the brunch selections to us. Do you know what's in the egg casserole?"

"Yup. Peppers, onions, and ham. I know because I helped Dad chop everything up. I even showed him Gran's trick to stop crying when you cut an onion. Do you know the trick, Mom?"

"I certainly do. Gran taught me the same trick."

Eventually, everyone gathered around the table in the dining room.

"Attention, please!" said Sam as he stood and clinked the end of his butter knife against the stem of his juice glass. "Before we start, I'd like to share a poem."

All chatter stopped as everyone focused their attention on Sam.

> "Two eyes to see you clearly
> Two ears to hear your voice
> Two arms to pick you up again,
> when you have no choice
> Two shoulders to lean on
> Two hands to wipe your tears
> Two feet to walk beside you,
> all through the years
> But, when it comes to mothers,
> there is only one
> to love, guide and support you,
> until the day is done."

"Sam, that was beautiful!" Maddie said as she blinked back a tear.

"I agree," said Stephanie.

"You do Pop proud," added Dean.

Maura stood and raised her glass. "I just want to say as the senior mom of this family that I couldn't be more impressed. I love you all more than I can put into words. Cheers to always honoring our family ties with continued respect, understanding, patience, and communication."

The family clinked glasses, aware of the bittersweet sentiment. After a long moment, they went back to eating and bantering until everyone had their fill.

While the boys cleared the table and the men cleaned the kitchen, Sally guided the women to the back deck, where she had set up a makeshift salon. She directed the ladies to sit at the outdoor bar, where a selection of nail polishes was displayed. "Welcome to Sally's Spa," she said with a sweeping arm gesture. "Please pick a nail polish and I will paint your fingernails. Mom said that if you already have a color on your nails, I can put on a clear coat."

"Since I don't have any nail polish on," Maura said, "you can paint mine this beautiful peach color."

"Very nice choice," said Sally as she climbed onto the barstool across from Maura.

"All done," said Sally when she finished. "Now just don't touch anything until they dry!"

"Yes, ma'am," said Maura as she slid off the stool to make room for Maddie.

She wandered onto the lawn where it was Kyle and Dean versus Jake and Sam in a game of cornhole.

"If Sam gets one more bean bag in, we win," Jake said.

Sam tossed the bag, made the point, and the boys beat the dads.

"We rule," said Sam, chest-bumping Jake.

Kyle tousled Jake's hair. "Yeah, yeah," he said as he fist-bumped Sam. "We'll get you next time."

For the remainder of the afternoon, the women relaxed while the children played. The men pampered them by making sure their glasses were full and requests tended to. All too soon, it was time for the celebration to come to an end.

Maura arrived back at home exhausted. She slid into bed and set her alarm. Through the open window, she could hear the familiar ting-a-ling of the wind chimes on the front porch. She stared into space and replayed the events of the day, her hands resting limply at her hips. She felt a pang of sadness as it occurred to her that Father's Day was just a few weeks away.

She rolled onto her side. The space that for so long had been filled with Paul's large frame felt like a vast hollow. She ran her hand along the spot where his body had lain next to hers for countless nights. She imagined the slight dip in his waistline where she would sometimes drape her arm when they spooned. She remembered the feel of his backside as she would press her thighs against him before she'd drift off to sleep, but sleep wouldn't come easily tonight.

* * * * * * * * * * * * * *

Eric and Maura found a seat in an open booth at a popular breakfast spot in town. It was Monday morning, time for Eric to collect on his bet.

"Will that class ever get any easier?" asked Eric.

"I hope not," joked Maura as she cut into her avocado toast.

Eric set his coffee on the table. "Saturday was a great time. Beth and Jimmy are so generous to host every year."

"Yes, and knock on wood," said Maura as her knuckles tapped her temple, "it's never rained." She paused before diving into uncharted waters. "So tell me, why haven't you ever brought someone special to any of our get-togethers?"

Eric smirked. "To be honest, I thought about it once, but when I mentioned it, the woman I was seeing was intimidated about meeting the group." He chuckled. "Not everyone is exercise-obsessed like we are. Honestly, I haven't met anyone worth pressing the subject."

Maura stopped sliding her coffee cup from one hand to the other and raised it to her lips in an effort to conceal her giddy grin.

"Thanks for the delicious meal," Eric said, after swallowing the last mouthful of his egg-and-salmon sandwich.

"Glad you enjoyed it, because next year you'll be treating me!"

They made their way out of the diner and onto the sidewalk. A light rain was falling. Eric reached into his backpack and pulled out a small black collapsible umbrella. "Here, take this," he said as he handed it to Maura. You can return it to me the next time I see you at the gym."

Maura gave him a surprised look. "Has anyone ever confused you with MacGyver?"

"When you travel as much as I do, it's second nature to be prepared for anything."

"Thanks. I'll make sure to put it in my gym bag." Then she gave him a quick hug goodbye.

After a busy weekend, Maura was happy for a day of solitude. She filled the hours with housework, food shopping, and errands. Thankless work, all of it, but undeniably satisfying at the end of the day to have a clean house, an empty clothes hamper, and a full fridge. As Maura had often thought, it was the best job she never had!

CHAPTER 18

"You can't make up for lost time.
You can only do better in the future."

— Ashley Ormon

"Hi, Maura," said Nicole. "Lonnie and I are debriefing our exciting Monday night." She wrestled her overstuffed gym bag from the locker.

"I let her talk me into a speed dating event Saturday night," said Lonnie. "To say it was pathetic would be an understatement."

"We can't decide which was worse," said Nicole, laughing so hard she had to catch her breath. "The selection of guys or the fact that we were there."

"As the saying goes, even a blind squirrel eventually finds a nut!" Maura said. "Don't give up hope, girls." She dug through her gym bag in search of shampoo and conditioner. As she turned toward the showers, she noticed Nicole suddenly huddling with Kara.

"Maura, come here," called Kara. "Jack and I met with Nicole over the weekend, and we listed our house. She's going to hold a realtors' open house on Thursday. The plan is to get the house on the market by the weekend."

"I told them now is the time of year to sell," said Nicole. "Families like to get settled before the school year begins, and as you know, they live in a desirable area. I'm sure it will sell quickly."

"Wow! Things are moving right along," said Maura. "At least we know you're in good hands. Have you and Jack started looking for a new place yet?"

"We plan to start this weekend. It's all very exciting. A little scary but exciting at the same time."

"I get it. Hey, sorry to change the topic, but have either of you seen Josie this morning—or yesterday, for that matter? I'm getting a little worried. It's not like her to skip the gym for so many days."

Neither Kara nor Nicole had seen Josie since Friday.

"I'll give her a call to make sure she's all right," said Maura. "But right now, I'm going to get cleaned up. I'm beginning to smell myself."

"Well, we are in a gym locker room," said Nicole. "It's understandable."

"Text us after you touch base with Josie," called Kara.

"Will do."

After a quick shower, she jumped into her clothes and exited the gym, anxious to reach out to Josie.

"Hey, Eric!" Maura shouted as she spotted him across the parking lot. She dipped her hand into her bag, found what she was searching for, and waved it in the air as she made her way to his car. "Thanks again for the loan."

"My pleasure." He reached for the umbrella, his hand brushing against hers.

Maura felt a quick surge of energy that startled her. She'd never thought of Eric in a romantic way, but the idea didn't displease her.

"It's great to see you," he said, "but I've got to run. Chamber of Commerce meeting at nine."

"Of course. Don't let me hold you up." She gave him a quick once-over and grinned. "By the way, you clean up well!"

"Who knew?" he said as he opened his car door and slid into the front seat.

Back in her car, Maura called Josie.

"Hi, Maura," Josie said flatly.

"Hi. We've missed you at the club. Is everything all right?"

"I just haven't felt like working out the past few days." Josie sighed. "Remember I told you about losing Diane," she said as more of a statement than a question. "The anniversary of her death was on Saturday. Some years it hits me harder than others."

"I'm so sorry, Josie. Listen, it's a beautiful day. What's your schedule like?"

"I'm finished at four."

"Why don't we meet at the park gazebo at four thirty? We can go for a walk and grab an early dinner."

"That would be lovely. I'll see you then."

* * * * * * * * * * * * * *

Maura and Josie strolled along the bike path.

"Have you ever noticed that spring, like fall, seems to peak?" Josie said. "In the fall, it's obvious. The leaves are at their brightest. But Diane pointed out once that there is a moment during spring when everything pops. Greens are their most verdant. Forsythia bushes beam. Flowering tree buds are as white as snow or as pink as cotton candy. Take a look around. We're just on the cusp of its ending."

Maura took in her surroundings. "I must admit, I don't think I ever actually noticed, but you're right. All the colors are so vivid."

"Diane was like that. She had a way of seeing and appreciating things that others take for granted. When she graduated from college, she joined the Peace Corps and spent two years in the South Pacific teaching high-school science. She said her experience there shaped the rest of her life. She learned to appreciate the beauty and value of people and experiences rather than things." Josie's eyes misted over. "She felt so strongly about the Peace Corps' impact that she convinced me. We even committed to joining as a couple—after we retired."

"Do you think you'll still do it on your own?"

"I don't think so. Diane had a way of nudging me out of my comfort zone." She wrinkled her nose. "From the time I hit puberty, my height made me self-conscious. I always felt like I stood out in a crowd." She pushed aside a strand of fringy blue bang that had slipped over her eye, and it shot back into place. "I've been to enough therapy to recognize that it's why I'm a bit of a loner. You girls are the first group of friends that I've had in years. I'm not that outgoing." She stopped mid-stride. "The thought of heading off to a foreign country on my own is inconceivable. Long story short, joining The Coastal

Club was a stretch for me."

Maura directed a smile at Josie as they began to stroll again. "Well, I know I speak for all of us when I say that we're glad you did."

As they made their way into town, Josie turned her attention to Maura. "Do you think you'll ever be able to love again after Paul?"

Maura was startled by the question. "Obviously, not yet, but I hope I'll be ready to try again someday. It's interesting how you knew right away that Diane would be your last love. To be honest, what Paul and I had was not at all what you two had, but I liked being half of a couple, and I think at some point in the future I'd like to be part of one again."

Over pizza and beer, they gabbed about love and loss, and after dinner, they embarked on a slow journey back to their cars, the scents of spring more pungent due to the dampness in the air. The sky had turned a pale pink by the time they reached the lot.

"Thank you so much for suggesting this, Maura. It's just what I needed."

"I must say, I think I did too. It's been nice to talk to someone else who's dealt with the loss of a spouse."

As she pulled out of the parking lot, Maura rolled down her window. "Hey, I expect to see you in the locker room tomorrow!"

Josie flashed a thumbs-up and a hopeful smile.

* * * * * * * * * * * * *

Maura no sooner entered her kitchen after Wednesday morning's spin class than the doorbell rang. She rushed to the foyer and pulled open the door to find a stocky, weathered older man and a lanky younger man with a beard and baseball cap.

"Hello, Mrs. Antonelli. I'm Don from the pool company. If it's all right with you, me and Steve here will head to the backyard and get started."

"Sure, just let me know if you need anything."

Second only to baseball's opening day, this was an event Paul counted down to every year—the pool-cover removal. It meant summer was finally here. Often, when grown children left home, backyard pools sat stagnant, but Maura and Paul had taken a dip every chance they could. She sighed. *Another shared activity she would have to do solo.*

She returned to the kitchen and peered out of the window as Don and Steve worked. Once again, unexpected grief punched her in the gut.

* * * * * * * * * * * * *

By the time Maura entered Lydia's parlor later that day, she felt grounded.

"Hello, Maura. How are you feeling today?"

"Better now. But once again, I was overcome with emotion unexpectedly. The pool was opened today, and it struck me that Paul won't be here to enjoy the summer and everything that goes with it: barbecues, family time…" Maura's eyes drifted to an invisible spot in the distance, and she continued in an exasperated tone. "See? I can talk about it now, but when I looked out the window and saw that crystal-blue water sparkling, it broke my heart."

"That's natural. It's all part of the grieving process. You

just have to ride it out and allow yourself to feel whatever you feel at that moment." She reached for the pitcher of water and poured them each a glass. "Are you ready to start?"

Maura took a gulp of water. "I am."

"Last week, we talked about the parts of yourself that you lost. This week, let's talk about what you've gained." She smiled at Maura. "You described yourself as responsible, supportive, and a problem solver. Those are important assets to have when moving forward on a new path. How does the phrase 'moving forward on a new path' make you feel?"

Maura pondered for a moment before responding, then smiled. "You've made me recognize that much of what I've done for the last thirty years has been reactive. Now that I'm in the driver's seat, I'm not even sure I want to take a new route, but the idea that I can is both exhilarating and scary."

"I'm sure it is, and maybe you don't ever want to change course. That's okay because what you've done and what you are doing has value. I wonder, though, if you've realized that if you do take a chance on something new, it's just a matter of having faith and putting yourself first—something you could have done before now. You are the same person with the same abilities."

"I guess I never thought of it that way. I've been swallowing my feelings of resentment for what I gave up—or could have been—for so long that I never pictured myself that way. To revisit the driving metaphor, I put up my own roadblocks." Unexpectedly, her eyes pooled with tears. "It's a shame that it took Paul's death to make me realize that these were my choices, not his, and not the kids' ultimatums. If I really want to be honest, it was safer to entrench myself in their successes or failures than to take chances of my own."

Lydia placed her hands on her knees and leaned in toward Maura.

"That's a major realization, one that many people never achieve. Now that you have, you must give yourself permission to explore the future you want to build. As I'm sure you know, life is about change. Whether we fight the change or embrace it is up to each of us. I want you to give yourself permission to embrace the change and take control of planning your future rather than waiting and reacting."

They spoke for another fifteen minutes until the session ended. "Our time is up for today," Lydia said, standing, "but I want you to know that what you are doing here is good, Maura."

"Thank you for walking through this with me. I'll see you next week."

* * * * * * * * * * * * *

The balmy May air complemented Maura's mood, so she decided to set the table on the screened porch. As she slipped the last of the crisp cotton napkins into the dainty mother-of-pearl napkin rings, she heard a voice call from inside."Hellooo!"

Maura recognized the voice immediately. "Stephanie! What a nice surprise. What are you doing here?"

"Kyle and his friend Jackson took the kids out for dinner. A new burger place they've been dying to try. I was on my way home from work, so I thought I'd stop by and see if you wanted to grab a bite." Without skipping a beat, she continued. "I assume you didn't check your email today; the DNA results are in."

Oh no, Anna is about to get very real.

There was a quick rapping, and the door opened again.

"Hi, Stephanie!" said Kara as she entered. "I didn't expect to see you tonight. What a great surprise."

"Hi, Kara!" She turned to Maura. "I forgot it's Wednesday, and you're having your gym ladies over."

As Kara and Stephanie caught up with each other, Maura got her heart rate back under control. "Honey, you're more than welcome to join us."

"That's okay. I'll leave you ladies to yourselves." She said her goodbyes, and as quickly as she'd appeared, she was gone.

"Maura, are you all right?" asked Kara. "You have a strange expression on your face."

The front door opened again, and Josie, Lonnie, and Nicole entered the now-cramped foyer.

Lonnie glanced at Maura and looked alarmed. "What's going on, Maura?"

"Stephanie just announced that the DNA results are in."

"Is Anna on the report?" asked Nicole, her voice hinting at excitement.

"I don't know. I haven't had a chance to look yet."

Josie locked eyes with her. "Grab your laptop; we'll all look at it together."

Maura flashed a lopsided smile. "I'll meet you on the screened porch," she said, heading upstairs to retrieve her laptop.

CHAPTER 19

"The time for action is now.
It's never too late to do something."

— Antoine de Saint-Exupéry

The idea of facing a new day was as appealing as root canal. Maura hit snooze and escaped into a deep slumber. Hours passed before she woke again. Unable to shake the gloomy feeling mushrooming inside of her, she made a cup of coffee, climbed back into bed, and spent the next few hours lost in a reality-show trance.

It was lunchtime before she descended the stairs again. She poured herself an iced tea, pulled out some leftovers, and stood at the island picking through the Tupperware containers.

I can't believe Anna didn't even show up in the DNA test results. If I'd kept my mouth shut, the kids would never have known.

Maura plunged a drumstick into a pool of sweet sticky

sauce and gnawed off a huge piece of barbecued chicken. *No, it's better that they know the truth.* She scooped a pile of coleslaw onto her fork and shoved it in her mouth.

Better for whom? she mused as she dipped and then chomped on the drumstick again. *What will Dean and Stephanie do next? We've already told the grandkids. I'm sure they'll try to contact her, but how?*

Maura slathered a piece of cornbread with butter and sunk her teeth into the slightly sweet, cake-like delight.

And what if they do find her? How will Anna react? Will she be thrilled to meet her half-siblings? She took a swig of iced tea. *Stephanie is clearly excited at the prospect of a half-sister.*

She shoveled another forkful of coleslaw into her mouth. *What if Anna is resentful that Dean and Stephanie got to grow up with the father she never knew? What if she wants to make them pay for living the life she never had a chance to live?*

"Stop it!" she yelled aloud, startled by the sound of her voice.

Unable to stuff another morsel into her body, she sat at the table and stared at the pie charts clipped to the fridge. Lydia's voice sounded in the back of her head: Maura, you can't go back in time and undo what's been done, so try to relax and wait for Dean and Stephanie's next move.

Lost in thought, it took Maura a moment to realize her cell phone was signaling a call.

"Hi, Steph."

"Hi. If you're free, Dean and I would like to meet you for dinner. We want to run something by you."

"Of course," she replied.

Unsure whether it was an aftereffect of gorging herself or a result of anxiety, Maura was overcome with a wave of nausea.

* * * * * * * * * * * * *

At six o'clock, Maura entered Murphy's and passed the bar filled with Yankees fans who were complaining about the Red Sox and the upcoming game slated to start soon. She spotted Stephanie and Dean at a table under a wall-mounted television in the corner.

"I just love this place, don't you?" asked Stephanie when Maura joined them. "I don't even have to look at the menu."

It wasn't long before a server arrived with two colossal Reuben sandwiches and an anemic dinner salad.

Maura picked at her salad while Dean and Stephanie covered the usual topics: kids and work. When she could wait no longer, she addressed the eight-hundred-pound gorilla in the room.

"I saw that Anna didn't appear on the DNA report."

"Crazy, isn't it?" said Dean. "Steph and I have been going back and forth about what to do. We've debated the pros and cons of reaching out to her." He bit into his gargantuan sandwich, and a dollop of Russian dressing spilled onto his plate. "On the plus side, we would get to meet our half-sister. It took a lot of cajoling from Stephanie to make me see that she's not just Dad's other daughter; she is our sister." He washed down his sandwich with a gulp of beer. "However, maybe she doesn't even know we exist. Or maybe she has no interest in forming a connection with us."

Stephanie took up where he'd left off. "If she knows about Dad, there's a good chance she'll be bitter about him turning his back on her while raising us. But it's a chance we're willing to take. In the end, we've decided that we would be no better than Dad if we don't reach out to her."

She turned and gazed at Dean; he nodded his head.

Focusing again on Maura, Stephanie continued. "As long as you are okay with it, we're planning to contact Anna."

Maura felt like the air had been sucked out of the room, but she stifled a gasp as she dabbed her mouth with her napkin. "Of course I'm all right with it," she fibbed. "I told you from the beginning that I'll support whatever decision you make."

"As soon as Steph and I decided," said Dean, "I did some internet searches. As luck would have it, Dad's high school friend Tommy sent both of us sympathy cards."

"Yes, Tommy sent his condolences in a lovely note and asked for your addresses."

Even though life had gotten busy, Maura knew that Paul and Tommy had kept in touch through social media, but it never occurred to her that he could be a connection to Anna.

"When I called him," said Dean, "he told me several stories about when he and Dad were kids." Dean smiled. "I could have recited them along with him. Dad told me the same stories so many times. Anyway, he gave me Anna's last name—Anderson. She took her stepfather's name when he adopted her."

Deep breaths, Maura reminded herself as she began to feel warm.

"Tommy also told me that Anna and her parents moved to upstate New York when she was young. With a general location, her name, her parents' names, and the year of her birth, it wasn't hard to connect the dots." He took a gulp of beer, then locked eyes with Maura. "Mom, I found her. She lives in Manhattan."

Maura felt lightheaded and released an audible sigh. "Wow! I wasn't expecting to hear that!" Now it was Maura who took a gulp of beer. "What's your next step?"

"We are going to reach out to her, explain that we are related, and ask her if she'd like to connect," said Stephanie.

"It certainly sounds like you two are determined to move forward with this."

Maura reached across the table and extended her open palms. Dean and Stephanie each grasped one of them.

"I am so proud of you for opening your hearts and taking a risk. I know this hasn't been easy for you." She released their hands and raised her glass. "A toast to the future, whatever it may bring."

They clinked glasses and spent the remainder of the dinner pondering what that future might bring.

* * * * * * * * * * * * * *

On Friday morning, Maura dragged herself into the locker room.

"My goodness, girl, you look like you just came out of battle," said Lonnie as Maura plopped down on a bench beside her.

"I'll tell you, Lonnie, these workouts never get any easier, but I love them."

"Whose turn is it to cook the family dinner tonight?"

"Actually, family dinner has been canceled this week. There's a school fundraiser that both families are going to, so I'm solo tonight."

Lonnie's eyes widened. "Then join me and Nicole for drinks and snacks at Salsa. They have a great happy hour.

We're meeting there at five thirty. It's always fun. They have a new drink special every hour and a really fresh taco bar." She bent down and slipped a gray mule onto her foot. "Afterward, we're going to The Art House to see a foreign film." She turned her gaze back to Maura. "Why don't you come?"

"Why not? I'll see you at five thirty."

While showering, Maura tried to remember the last time she went out for a Friday happy hour, let alone a movie at The Art House.

When she was raising the kids, it wasn't an option. and because she didn't work, Friday had become just like any other day. Contrary to the old song lyric, she wasn't working for the weekend, and Paul was happy to put his feet up on a Friday night and relax. She left the gym eagerly anticipating a night out on the town.

* * * * * * * * * * * * *

By the time Maura pulled into Salsa's parking lot, her excitement had turned into anxiety. Paul had always driven when they went out, and he'd always pointed out a place to sit or stand once they entered a bar.

Stop it! Just take a breath, put on your big girl pants, and go in there. You've got this.

She entered the restaurant and darted toward an empty barstool. She hoisted herself up, hung her bag on the knee-level hook in front of her, and was startled to hear a familiar voice coming from the stool next to hers.

"Come here often?" Eric asked in a playfully snarky tone before waving at the bartender. "Bill, I'll have another beer.

What would you like?"

"Oh my gosh, Eric, hi. I'd love a beer. Thanks."

"Make it two beers. Thanks, Bill."

"Hi, guys," Nicole called as she and Lonnie approached.

"Hi," said Maura. "I didn't know you two knew each other." She was surprised by a fleeting proprietorial pang in her chest.

"We're fellow Chamber of Commerce members. They couldn't manage without us," Eric said, winking at Nicole.

Lonnie extended a hand. "Hi, I'm Lonnie."

"Nice to meet you, Lonnie. What are you ladies drinking?"

The foursome shifted to a high-top table and shared stories and laughs.

"You're right, Lonnie, this taco bar is amazing," Maura said. "Thanks so much for including me tonight. And Eric, I'm so glad we ran into you."

"I'll toast to that!" Eric said, gesturing to the bartender from afar. "Bill, four shots of tequila."

The women gorged themselves on tacos while Eric regaled them with tales of his travels. He laughed at himself easily, a quality Maura found endearing.

They all took one last shot to toast the idea of taking a trip together. Eric would plan the itinerary, and they would invite Beth and Jimmy, plus the supper club.

"I hate to be Debbie Downer," said Nicole, "but the movie starts in twenty-five minutes."

"Excuse me," said Maura, "I need to run to the restroom before we go." As she stood, the room seemed to tilt a bit. She clutched the table to stop the motion. "I'm a little woozy. Guess I'm more of a lightweight than I realized."

Eric squeezed her arm gently and slid a glass toward her.

"Here, have some water." He jumped up and returned with a bowl of nacho chips. "Munch on these; they'll help you feel better."

"You know what?" Maura said, sitting back down. "I think maybe I'll skip the movie."

Eric turned to Lonnie and Nicole. "Why don't you ladies go ahead? I'll sit here with Maura for a while and then drive her home."

"Is that okay with you?" said Nicole. "We can stay too."

"No," Maura said, "you go ahead. As long as you don't mind, Eric?"

"Of course not." Eric stood and hugged Nicole goodbye. "Lonnie, it was great to meet you. This was fun! Let's do it again soon."

"I'm so embarrassed," said Maura after the girls had gone. "Thanks for staying with me."

"Hey, it happens. I'll order us each a double espresso, and you can tell me all about your favorite vacation."

Unsure if it was the alcohol or Eric's easy manner, but Maura told him about all of the places she'd read about but never visited.

"From the time I was young, I kept a travel diary, not of where I'd been but of where I wanted to go. I used to make up itineraries and list the tourist attractions, museums, and monuments I wanted to visit. I'd even list the foods I wanted to sample in each place."

"That's wonderful. When you're ready, you can pick one of those places and follow your dreams. I think traveling to new places and experiencing different cultures is one of the best gifts we can give ourselves."

Maura grinned, finding Eric's enthusiasm contagious.

"Oh my gosh," she said, glancing at the clock over the bar. "I can't believe how late it's gotten!"

"You ready to go?"

"Yes, and I think I'm okay to drive now. Sorry about drinking too much," she whispered as her cheeks flushed to pink.

"Maura, it's me you're talking to. Please don't ever feel embarrassed around me. We've known each other far too long. Do you know you were one of the first people I met when I joined The Coastal Club? It's been ten years now." His eyebrows arched. "The first class I ever took was Extreme Boot Camp, and I had no idea how intense it would be. You helped me set up my station, and the rest is history." He shook his head. "I was hooked."

"Oh my gosh, I forgot all about that!"

He smiled. "You sure you're okay?"

She stood and scanned the room; she was able to focus without the room spinning. In fact, the only thing she felt was a slight throbbing in her temple.

"I'm fine, really."

"Okay, then come on. I'll walk you to your car." He grinned. "I guess I can beat you at handling liquor too!"

* * * * * * * * * * * * * *

Maura dragged herself out of bed and made her way to the kitchen. Before long, she shuffled to the screened porch with a cup of coffee and a plate of food, and dug in. It was amazing what fresh air and caffeine could do to revive a person. *Of course, this pork roll, egg, and cheese sandwich doesn't hurt either!*

As she took another bite, her phone sounded. She quickly swallowed the salty, gooey delight and answered the call.

"Good morning," said Eric. "I hope you're up and at 'em today because I have a proposition."

"Sounds intriguing."

"To be honest, I feel guilty for plying you with alcohol and causing you to miss the movie. I get off work at five today. How about we go to see the movie at five thirty, then grab some dinner afterward? My treat—no alcohol."

Maura contemplated the offer. She couldn't think of a reason not to. "My inability to handle that much alcohol is not your responsibility. That said, I'd love to go, but I insist on splitting the bill. I'm a big girl, and I could've said no to a drink at any time."

"Fair enough. How about I meet you at the theater at five-fifteen?"

"Perfect."

After the call, Maura immediately identified the rumble in her stomach as excitement but decided to devour the rest of her sandwich just in case.

* * * * * * * * * * * * * *

The Art House theater was a small venue. Donors helped subsidize it, and volunteers ran the projection room and snack bar. In this particular screening room, donated recliners were lined up in three rows of four. It was an intimate way to watch foreign, independent, and cutting-edge films. This weekend's selection was a French film with subtitles about a couple who had drifted apart and taken lovers. After their adolescent daughter found out what they had been up to, they were forced to reckon with the fallout of their choices, and a bittersweet story ensued.

Eric and Maura settled into their seats as the lights went down, and for an hour and a half, Maura was engrossed in the film. It was visually stunning and emotionally heart-wrenching. The lights came up to reveal Eric dragging the cuff of his sleeve across his eye.

He caught Maura's gaze and chuckled as he blushed. "Hey, I'm all man! I just happen to have a sensitive side."

Maura patted him on the arm. "It's refreshing to see a man in touch with his sensitive side. Come on, let's go. I'm starving!"

They decided to go to Harry's Place, and although the bar was packed, they got a table quickly.

"Hi, I'm Angie. Can I get you something to drink while you decide on dinner?"

"I'll have a glass of your house cab," Maura said, winking at Eric. "Trust me; there won't be a repeat of last night."

"Angie, make that two, thanks."

Over dinner, they deconstructed the movie.

"I just love movies with subtitles," said Maura. "They're the best of both worlds. You get to read the story and see the action in living color."

"What I love about foreign films is how the directors aren't afraid of silence. Musical scores don't dictate the mood like they do in most American films."

"I agree! And I love how there's often more conversation than action. I feel like I'm spying on someone's most intimate moments, thoughts, and feelings."

"Not to mention the scenery."

"I couldn't agree more. At least, if I can't get there in

person, I can visit through films!"

They continued to talk even after the bill had been settled and the table cleared.

"Now that I know you love foreign films," Eric said, "we'll have to make a point to catch them when they come to town. They're not for everyone. As a matter of fact, I don't know anyone else who loves them as much as I do. And I'll let you in on a little secret."

"Do tell."

"I usually go to see them by myself."

"Paul was not a fan, and it never occurred to me to go to a movie by myself."

"Well then, not only will we be workout buddies, we will be film partners as well."

"Agreed," said Maura as Eric walked her to her car for the second time that weekend.

CHAPTER 20

"All we have to decide is what to do with the time that is given us."

— J. R. R. Tolkien

Sunday slipped away, and Maura was surprised when she realized it was time for dinner. She opened the freezer and snagged a container of bean-and-escarole soup. She dumped the soup into a pot on the stove, made a simple salad of romaine lettuce, and drizzled olive oil on top. Then she added a squeeze of fresh lemon and a sprinkle of shaved parmesan before placing it in the fridge. She poured a glass of sparkling water and went to the family room to read the newspaper until the soup was heated. Saturday's travel section was always her first choice. As she read, she was reminded of sharing the story of her travel diary with Eric. It was so strange how the supper club girls and Eric had been her friends for years, but she was only getting to know them now.

Her train of thought was derailed by her cell phone ringing. She grabbed it off the ottoman and answered. “Hi, Steph, what's up?”

“Mom, you won’t believe it. Anna got back to us and said she’d love to meet us! Dean and I are getting together with her in Manhattan in two weeks!”

“That was fast,” she said as her pulse quickened.

“Anna asked if we could bring some pictures of Dad, and you too. Okay if I grab some on Friday? I’m sure the kids will like going through them.”

Maura’s mind raced as fast as her pulse. “Yes, of course.” She focused on keeping her rising panic from spilling into her voice. “Are you going to bring the kids to meet her?”

“No. This meeting will be just Dean and me. If all goes well, and she’s interested, then we’ll introduce her to the whole gang—Mom, I’m so excited! I will get to meet the sister I’ve always wanted.”

Maura knew she should just listen and be supportive, but as a mother, she couldn’t help but give unsolicited advice. “Steph, be careful, and take it slow. You don’t know anything about her, and this may be difficult for her. She didn’t get to grow up with Dad like you did.”

“I know, Mom. I’m not a child.”

“I’m sorry. I just don’t want anyone to get hurt. By the way, how does Dean feel about meeting Anna?”

“In true Dean manner, he is approaching this in a logical, detached way, the same way he approaches any situation he can’t control.”

“At least he’s not being resistant like he was at first.”

They said their goodbyes, and Maura headed to the kitchen. She turned off the pot of soup, opened the fridge, and grabbed a bottle of pinot grigio, replacing her sparkling water with wine. Then she pulled out a block of sharp cheddar and placed it on the scarred wooden cutting board on the island. From the pantry, she grabbed a box of crackers, then lifted herself onto a stool.

She swallowed the chilled wine, cut a chunk of cheese, and placed it on a cracker. After a second gulp of wine, she felt her cheeks warm, and she closed her eyes.

"Paul!"

She refilled her glass and drank until she felt numb. Leaning her elbows on the island, she rested her head in her hands.

After a long while, she sat up in the semi-dark kitchen that now had a muddy hue. She got up and mindlessly wandered toward the foyer, leaving the wine and cheese out. Then she climbed the stairs and coiled up on the bed.

Hours passed before music from a passing car awakened her. She slipped out of her clothes, climbed between the sheets, and stared at the ceiling until sleep came again.

* * * * * * * * * * * * *

By the time Maura entered Lydia's parlor on Wednesday afternoon, she was beside herself. "Oh, Lydia, I don't think I can handle this."

"I'm listening. Tell me what's happening."

"Dean and Stephanie have located Anna." Her voice increased in volume. "They're meeting with her this weekend."

"Take a deep breath, Maura. You knew this was a possibility. What are you afraid of?"

"What am I afraid of?" Her eyebrows slid up her forehead, her head rotating from right to left. The thought of Dean and Stephanie being hurt emotionally by Anna was almost more than she could bear. "What if Anna is bitter about not being raised by Paul? Dean and Stephanie are so open to connecting with her, and I can't imagine how they'll feel if she harbors animosity toward them—all because of Paul's choice. And what if she has ulterior motives? What if she's connecting with them so she can play on their heartstrings?" She swung the foot of her crossed leg like a metronome set to a high rate. "Maybe she'll lay a guilt trip on them so she can ask them for money." The tempo of her words aligned with the pulsing of her foot. "What if she's planning something even more sinister than that? I mean, really, we know nothing about this woman. She may have spent her entire life resenting all of us!"

Maura ran her fingers through her hair, from the front of her scalp to the back, twice before continuing. "Do you remember that famous court case? From the nineties? A Ken and Barbie couple married after graduating college. She went to work and supported them while he went to law school. Then they had a slew of kids and she stayed home and took care of the brood, became the team mother, the scout leader, and all that." Maura shrugged her shoulders. "And put on a few pounds in the process. Meanwhile, her husband took up with a hot twenty-something who worked in his office and eventually married her. To say the first wife was bitter is an understatement, but at least she had the kids on her side—that was until the newlyweds won them over. The first wife got so angry that she broke into their house one night and shot them both dead!" She looked pleadingly at Lydia. "Resentment can cause people to do crazy things."

Lydia got up and went to the antique secretary desk nestled in the corner of the room. She retrieved a pen and a composition book and placed them on the coffee table.

"Maura, I think your anxiety stems more from your anger at Paul than from the idea of Dean and Stephanie meeting with Anna. They have proven to you that they are resilient, and they've shown you that they're a good support system for each other. But remember, you chose not to have any more children with Paul without telling him. You gave up your career in order to perpetuate a lie."

Maura listened to Lydia, eyes down, picking at a fingernail.

"I think it's time you tell Paul how you really feel about the choices he made—and share with him the choices you made so you can finally move on."

Maura glanced up, tilted her head, and furrowed her brow.

"I want you to write Paul a letter. Tell him everything you've been holding inside for the past thirty-plus years. It's about time he knows the truth!"

Lydia pushed the pen and notebook closer to Maura, who stared at them for several moments before picking them up and writing. When the letter was complete, she tore it from the notebook and placed it on the table. She let out an audible puff of air, then looked up to see that Lydia had rearranged the two wing chairs so that they now faced each other.

Lydia instructed Maura to sit in one chair and picture Paul in the other. Maura moved to one of the chairs.

"Now read the letter aloud to Paul."

Maura picked up the letter in her trembling hands and read aloud:

"Dear Paul,

"I have to tell you something. Something I should have shared with you long before this. The truth is, I feel that unless I get this off my chest, I won't be able to move on with my life.

"As you know, we wanted to have a large family. When you cried after Dean's birth, I thought you were shedding tears over the arrival of our son and the loss of the daughter you gave up. You seemed so vulnerable. That might have been the moment that I loved you the most.

"I'm sure you remember how things between us changed after I gave birth to Stephanie. When I explained that I was overwhelmed by raising two children, I was lying. I was really overwhelmed with anger. What may have looked to you like aloofness was in fact resentment.

"When I saw you hold our little girl for the first time, all I could think about was Anna. I couldn't fathom what kind of father could just walk away from his child and carry on as if she didn't exist. It made me sick, and I made a decision right then and there to never have any more children with you, so I went on birth control without telling you. I pretended to be overwhelmed by raising two children, and I gave up my career to dote on you and our family.

"Since you've been gone, I've taken a lot of time to reflect. Looking back on my decision and our life together, I realize how angry I was for so many years. In my mind, I quickly fell into the role of victim, and I wore that title like an invisible badge of honor. I was so proud of myself for playing the part of the dedicated mother and supportive wife, but inside I was seething with resentment for not continuing my career and not having the family I wanted.

"Now I see my choices in a different light, and I no longer feel anger. What I feel is regret. Regret for what was, regret for what could have been. Paul, I can honestly say I loved you until the end. You were a wonderful provider and father; however, after Stephanie's birth, I was no longer in love with you, and I know over time, you fell out of love with me. It makes me wonder what would have happened if I had been honest with you from the start. I guess I'll never know.

"Our children are about to meet your other daughter. I've been so livid with you for leaving me behind to pick up the pieces of your broken past. However, I am beginning to

> see that it's not your broken past I should focus on. Instead, I should build a future with our children and their half-sister. I'm tired of allowing resentment to guide me.
>
> "For the first time in a long time, I am dictating my path. I am taking back ownership of my actions and reactions."

She stopped reading and looked at Lydia, her cheeks glistening.

"Maura, repeat after me: Paul, I forgive you for your choices."

Maura plucked a tissue from the box and dabbed her cheeks. "Paul, I forgive you for your choices."

"I forgive myself for my choices."

"I forgive myself for my choices," Maura repeated softly.

"I know that was difficult, but you are stronger than you know. The fact that you were able to move from anger to regret is monumental. Just like you are mourning Paul's death, you are now free to mourn the death of your relationship."

They practiced new relaxation techniques, and then Lydia assigned Maura some homework. By the time Maura started her car, she felt optimistic. Writing that letter to Paul and then speaking her forgiveness aloud had opened a portal to the future.

As she turned onto her street, she became aware of an unfamiliar sound. It took a moment for her to realize it was her own voice. The radio was tuned to her favorite classic rock station, and she was belting out the lyrics of "You Can't Always Get What You Want" along with Mick Jagger. She pulled into the garage singing, "You just might find, you get what you need."

CHAPTER 21

"There's only one thing more precious than our time, and that's who we spend it with."

— Leo Christopher

"I just can't believe it's happening so quickly," said Kara as she squeezed a balled-up cocktail napkin at the next supper club. "One minute I'm excited, and the next I'm terribly sad. Our family had so many wonderful times in that house."

"What you are feeling is totally normal," said Nicole. "Our home is our safe place, where we retreat for shelter and comfort, and for most of us, it's our biggest financial investment. We move in and turn a house into a home, with everything that word symbolizes. We celebrate milestones, soldier through difficult times, and build traditions. And then, when we choose to sell, our focus shifts from it being our home back to it being a house. The bottom line becomes about money, and it can be hard to reconcile the two."

Nicole reached into her bag and pulled out three brochures. "Here are three adult communities you might want to consider." She passed them to Kara.

"Look them over and let me know if you'd like to see them. I've highlighted the models that are up for sale." She addressed the group. "Sorry to mix business with pleasure, ladies."

"Can I see those brochures?" said Josie.

Kara handed them over.

"Ah, this is where I live!" Josie said. "I'll text you my address. If you decide to look at a house there, stop by."

"I'll definitely take you up on that. Thanks."

"Come and get it," called Maura from the kitchen. "Tonight we feast on homemade pizza. Please help yourselves."

"Wednesday night dinner has become my favorite meal of the week," said Nicole as she chose a slice of pizza topped with smoked mozzarella, white bean bruschetta, prosciutto, and a drizzle of balsamic glaze."

"I know this is last minute," Maura said as they sat, "but if you're free on Sunday, my kids and their families are coming over for our annual Memorial Day party, and I'm feeling a little shaky. Paul and I used to work together all morning preparing, and once everyone arrived, he manned the grill. This will be my first time flying solo." She crossed her feet to quiet her legs. "It would mean the world if you could come. You've all become such rocks for me." Turning to Kara, she added, "You're more than welcome to bring your family. I'm sure the kids would love to catch up."

"That's a terrific idea," Kara said. "Trisha, Todd, and the kids are flying in on Saturday. We'll be happy to come."

"I think it's time for the rest of you to get to know my kids and grandkids," Maura said. "Heck, you've been hearing about them for years."

They all agreed to attend.

"Now," proclaimed Nicole as she lifted a slice of cheesy goodness from her plate, "let's get back to this pizza before it gets cold."

When everyone had gone, Maura climbed into bed, set her alarm, and turned off the bedside light. The cracked windows allowed the cool night air to chill the room. She burrowed under the covers, her body warm and the pillowcase cool as she drifted off to sleep.

* * * * * * * * * * * * * *

Anyone who lived at the Jersey Shore knew Memorial Day weekend could be a bang or a bust depending on the weather. Some years it was cold and rainy, others sunny and warm. Sunday morning was perfect—not a cloud in sight as Maura trotted down her driveway for a run. Sweat glistened on her bare arms and legs as she jogged through the neighborhood. Red, white, and blue bunting adorned several porches, and American flags flew en masse.

Six baskets filled with cool-green vinca vines and geraniums the color of her favorite pink lipstick hung from hooks on Maura's porch, while Old Glory hung limply from its pole. When she returned to her yard, she turned on the garden hose and cooled the back of her neck before giving the flowers a drink.

She finished in the front, then moseyed around to the back to water some more. Hot-pink hibiscus nestled between the lounge chairs lining the pool, and potted palms marked each corner of the gleaming white pool deck. Meanwhile, lush green ferns dangled from decorative holders inside the screened porch, flanking each of the support posts.

Her watering complete, she turned off the hose and entered the kitchen through the screened porch. Usually, she relished party prep, but that was when Paul worked by her side. Now all she could focus on was the rollercoaster careening around her stomach. *Hope I didn't bite off more than I can chew. What ever made me think I could throw this party on my own?*

Showered and dressed, she returned to the kitchen just as Sally, waving a small American flag, came running across the patio.

"Surprise!" she shouted as she burst into the kitchen. "We're all here to help with the party."

She wrapped her arms around Maura's waist.

Following close behind were Sam and Jake, each carrying an aluminum tray. "Jake has a pasta salad, and I have baked beans," said Sam.

"Place them on the island," said Maura, her crow's feet deepening as relief brought the rollercoaster to a screeching halt.

"Hey, Mom, let's get this party started," said Dean as he entered the kitchen carrying a pitcher of Bloody Marys and a stack of red plastic cups.

"He insisted," said Maddie, giving Maura a quick hug.

Kyle and Stephanie trailed behind, carrying ice.

"These are for you," said Stephanie, handing her mother a cluster of chalky white carnations in a ruby-red vase.

"They're beautiful! Put them out on the porch." Maura blinked, tears pooling in her eyes. "I didn't expect to see any of you until later."

"Come on, Mom, you didn't think we'd leave you hanging, did you?" said Dean as he handed Maura a Bloody Mary.

"I have to admit, I was feeling a little down this morning, but not anymore." She sipped her drink. "Just what the doctor ordered."

"Let's get to work," said Dean.

"I'll be in charge of the music, Gran," said Sam.

"Perfect. The outdoor speakers are in the basement on the shelf next to the dryer."

Maura turned to Jake and Sally. "Can you two shuck that basket of corn outside? Use the garbage can on the patio for husks."

Although Jersey corn wouldn't be available for several more weeks, the Florida corn from the local food store was always a favorite season-opener.

Kyle set up the drink station, and Dean declared himself grill master, but until needed, he took care of cleaning the porch and deck, inflating the new floats, and vacuuming the pool. Stephanie and Maddie worked with Maura to finish food prep and set up paper goods.

By one o'clock, they were ready to change into their swimsuits and put out snacks.

"Geez, I never realized how much work went into your parties," said Dean when they all convened back in the kitchen.

Maura gave his back a quick rub. "I can't thank you all enough for coming to help. I couldn't have done it without you."

At two o'clock, the first guests arrived. Stephanie greeted Kara, Jack, and their two grandchildren as they entered the backyard.

"Hi, everyone! Mom is in the kitchen. Kara, you can bring that bowl right inside. Oh my goodness, look how big—" Before she could finish, Kara's two grandchildren jumped into the pool to join Sam, Jake, and Sally in a game of Marco Polo.

Jack hugged Stephanie. "It's good to see you. I sure wish your Dad could be here with us. We had a lot of fun times together over the years."

"We sure did," said Stephanie as Jack released her.

"But one thing I know for sure is your Dad wouldn't want us to spend a glorious day like this sulking."

"You're right," Stephanie said with a nod. "By the way, where are Trisha and Todd?"

"They flew in late last night. We told them to sleep in while we took the grandkids out for breakfast and then to the boardwalk. They should be here soon."

A few minutes later, the back gate swung open again.

"Hi, everyone! I'm Nicole, and I've got an ice cream cake that's going to turn into an ice cream puddle if I don't get it into the freezer." She scurried inside.

Next, Lonnie pulled open the gate and scanned the backyard. She zeroed in on two young men who were sitting on the patio, sipping cold beer and snacking on nachos.

"Hi, I'm Lonnie," she said as she cradled a bowl of fruit salad in one arm and extended the other.

Dean jumped to his feet. "I'm Maura's son, Dean. It's nice to meet you." He gestured toward Kyle, who was now also standing. "And this is my brother-in-law, Kyle, but there'll be no handshakes." He leaned in and gave Lonnie a hug. "Mom refers to you ladies as family, so we will too."

Kyle followed suit.

"Well, my goodness," said Lonnie, "I should have known you would be as welcoming as your mom. Good to meet you both. I'm going to make my way inside to say hello to Maura."

Josie stopped just inside the gate to take in her surroundings. Bruce Springsteen's praise for his Jersey girl was competing with the shouts of "Marco" and "Polo" echoing forth from the pool.

"Hi, I'm Stephanie, we met briefly a few weeks ago, when you ladies were here for dinner."

"Yes, I remember. I'm Josie."

"Here, let me help you with that." Stephanie took the boxful of wine bottles from Josie's arms.

"Oh, thank you."

Stephanie directed Josie into the kitchen, where a group was huddled around Nicole's phone.

"He's cute, don't you think?" Nicole was saying. "His name is Harris. I'm meeting him later for a drink."

"Two dates in and no red flags so far," said Lonnie. "Seems promising—fingers crossed."

"Come on, ladies, it's much too nice out to be caught in here," said Maura as she led the group out of the kitchen and onto the screened porch.

The children cheered loudly as Kyle, Dean, and Todd competed in a cannonball competition to see who could make the biggest splash, while in the shallow end of the pool, Trisha and Stephanie bobbed in the waves, heads together, holding onto each other's floats like school girls talking about their latest crushes.

"Oh my gosh," exclaimed Trisha, "this is crazy. First, you had to deal with your Dad passing and now this." Eyebrows raised, chin tilted down. “How is our Dean dealing with this?” she asked out of the corner of her mouth.

“Only the third musketeer would ask that question!” said Stephanie as she squeezed Trisha’s arm.

Suddenly a body torpedoed into the pool, toppling the women off their floats and into the cool water.

“Dean!” they cried in unison.

“Hey, I thought I heard the three musketeers mentioned. Here I am, at your service.”

“Stephanie was just filling me in on the whole Anna situation.”

“It’s hard to believe, right?”

“Well, look at you three! I see nothing has changed,” Maura called from the pool deck. “I hate to break up the band, but Dean, would you mind starting the grill?”

“Sure thing,” he said as he waded to the stairs, but not before splashing the girls one last time.

* * * * * * * * * * * * *

Everyone seemed to find the meal scrumptious. Plates were piled high with hotdogs, hamburgers, salads, beans, and corn on the cob. By the time Nicole’s ice cream cake and Lonnie’s fruit salad were served, everyone claimed to be full, happy, and exhausted.

Josie and Lonnie announced that they would stay to help clean up, an offer Maura gladly accepted.

The women finished up in the kitchen just as the mahogany grandfather clock in the foyer chimed ten.

“That was a wonderful party. Thank you so much for including us,” said Josie as she returned from the family room with her bag and car keys.

"I'm so glad you all came."

"And what a wonderful family you have," said Lonnie.

Maura giggled nervously. "It's almost time to add one more person into the mix," she said as she held up two crossed fingers.

CHAPTER 22

"There's no time like the present."

— *English Proverb*

The next morning, Sally strutted down the annual Memorial Day parade route with her fellow Girl Scouts throwing handfuls of miniature Tootsie Rolls. "Gran!"

"Hi, Sally!" called Maura.

"She is so darn cute," said Beth. "I can't wait to have grandchildren, but I don't think my girls are ready."

Before Maura could respond, an antique car horn sounded. *Ahrugha*! Eric waved from behind the wheel. "I'll see you later!"

By three o'clock, Beth and Jimmy's backyard buzzed with activity.

"I don't know how you do it," said Eric as he delivered Jimmy a tray of marinated chicken breasts. "You just hosted us a few weeks ago, and here you go again."

"There's nothing we love more than a full house. Besides,

that's what summer is for: friends, food, and fun."

The afternoon passed in a flurry of activity, and by early evening, the party had wound down.

"Thanks for all your help today," said Beth to Maura as she placed the last remaining serving bowl in the dishwasher. "I think Jimmy and Eric are sitting on the patio. Jimmy made a fire. Would you like to hang out for a while?"

"I'd love to," said Maura.

Beth dipped her hand into the icy slush pooling on the bottom of the cooler and retrieved four bottles of water. Then she and Maura headed toward the guys.

"Thought you might like one of these," Beth said as she handed them each an ice-cold bottle.

"Thanks," said Eric. "Jimmy said summer is for friends, food, and fun. I for one had as much food and fun as I can handle today."

"I'm so happy we all agreed to do the Sea to Shore triathlon at the end of the summer!" said Beth. "It's been so long since I've done one."

"You're better off than me. I've never done one," admitted Eric. "What about you, Maura?"

"I haven't done one either, but I must admit I've always wanted to. It just always seemed so daunting. Did you know the ride and the run course go right by our house? Paul and I would sit on the front porch and cheer the racers on."

"Jimmy, why don't you sign up?" asked Eric.

"Someone has to be available to hand off the towels."

Eric turned to Beth. "How do we go about training?"

"We have ten weeks to get ready," said Beth. "We can follow a training plan on our own during the week, but it would be great if we could meet on Sundays to train together."

"I'm in!" said Eric.

"Me too," agreed Maura.

"I'll email a training plan tomorrow," Beth said.

"It's getting late, and this has been a long day," said Eric.

Maura stood and nodded in agreement. They said goodbye to their hosts and strolled to the street.

"Get some rest," called Eric as he and Maura got into their cars. "You're in training."

"Right back at you!"

Driving home, she realized that for the first time since Paul's death, she was focusing on the future instead of trying to merely get through the day.

* * * * * * * * * * * * *

After the busy weekend, Maura listened to Eric's advice and slept in. She woke to the sound of the bedroom blinds rattling and pulled the blanket up to her chin. The weather over the weekend had been clear, bright, and unseasonably hot, but today was damp, cloudy, and cold.

Her morning coffee, hot and rich, warmed her from the inside out as she sat at the kitchen desk and searched "sprint distance triathlon" on her laptop. She discovered that typically the swim was just under a half mile. *I can do that.* The bike ride was twelve-and-a-half miles. *Okay, that's doable.* And the run was just over three miles. *Heck, I can run five.* Then she bit her lip. The challenge would be doing it all, one after the other.

She checked for an email from Beth in hopes of finding a training plan. It was there, but so was a generic message from the DNA company, encouraging subscribers to expand their searches for a small fee.

She quickly deleted the message but couldn't erase the feeling of dread enveloping her. *Only one week until Dean and Stephanie meet Anna.* She closed her eyes. Lydia had suggested she focus on positive thoughts and scenarios to release her stress. She pictured her grandchildren frolicking in her pool and could feel herself relaxing.

She opened her eyes. *What am I worried about? What's the worst that could happen when they meet her? They can handle it. I raised strong, competent people, after all.*

* * * * * * * * * * * * *

As Maura slipped into the club pool, it dawned on her that she never opened Beth's email about the training plan. Since she knew that she could swim sixteen hundred yards, she decided to kick. She'd have to use her legs on the ride and the run, so it made sense that the stronger they were, the easier the ride and run would be.

After a warm-up swim, she slid each foot into a flipper and grabbed her kickboard. Her fins added resistance, and the kickboard made her more buoyant. For the remainder of her workout, she focused on building leg strength. The rest of the world vanished as she powered across the pool.

* * * * * * * * * * * * *

Wednesday morning spin class was almost over. A cacophony of grunts and sighs were emitted as the last effort came to an end. The playlist switched to a cooldown song as Maura's heart rate dropped and her breath came back under control.

"Hey, are you in there?" joked Eric as he handed off a spray bottle of cleaner to her.

"Thanks," said Maura as she wiped down her bike. "I'm just a little distracted today."

"Is everything okay?"

"Oh yeah, I'm fine. I just have some family stuff on my mind."

"Hey, what do you two think of the training plan?" called Beth from across the room.

"It looks good. I can't imagine the ride will be any harder than this class," said Eric.

"True," Beth said. "The challenge is doing it after the swim and before the run. Speaking of which, I was thinking we could meet for a long run on Sunday."

"Sounds good," said Maura. "Eric?"

"Absolutely."

* * * * * * * * * * * * *

Promptly at six thirty, Maura entered Harry's Place and realized she was the first of the supper club to arrive. She requested a table for five. A thin man with wavy gray hair and a blue polyester sport coat led her to a large booth. Neither the decor nor the menu at Harry's had changed in decades, but for a great burger or chop, the place couldn't be beat.

"Let me slide in next to you," said Nicole when she arrived, shimmying across the red leather bench.

"How are you?" Maura said. "Things working out with Harris?"

Nicole beamed. "I'm taking it slow, but I think this guy is a keeper!"

"Good evening, ladies, can I interest you in a drink?" inquired the server once the entire group had assembled.

He took their drink orders, but before he could walk away, Lonnie spoke up. "We'd also like an order of your onion ring loaf."

All eyes focused on Lonnie.

Nicole gasped. "Lonnie, are you sure?"

"I'm sure. This time, I've found a lifestyle, not a diet." She smiled at Maura, who responded with a wink and a grin. "Between my trainer, nutritionist, and therapist—thanks again for that recommendation, Josie—I've learned that I can eat everything. I just have to control how much. A few mouthfuls of fried, breaded, mouth-wateringly delicious onions won't send me into a tailspin. It's not heroin!"

The waiter returned with the drinks and onion loaf, and the women immediately tore the loaf to shreds.

Between mouthfuls, Nicole filled the group in on Harris. "He's easygoing and interesting, and he seems to be ticking off the items on my checklist, which, I might add, has changed recently."

Everyone stopped and stared.

"Let me explain. Until now, a man's looks and wallet were my priorities. But that hasn't been working for me. So I did some soul-searching and realized that what I really want is someone who is smart, kind, and easy to be with—with no baggage. I don't need to jump into someone else's crazy. Once I realized that, it was like the universe sent Harris to me. I bumped into him in the coffee shop. Literally. I spilled my iced coffee on him, and we started talking. I've seen him three times now, and we haven't even kissed! There's definitely chemistry, but as I said, I'm taking it slow, and I guess he is too. But enough about me. Kara, I've set up an appointment to show you a house in Josie's community on Saturday at one. Does that work for you?"

"Works for me, but Jack has a charity golf outing." She turned to Maura. "Would you come with me? I don't want to pass up a chance to see the house, and I'd love a second set of eyes."

"Absolutely! Saturday is when Dean and Stephanie are meeting Anna, so spending the day with you would be a blessing. If I sit at home alone, I'll go out of my mind."

"How about stopping by my place afterward?" said Josie. "Lonnie, you come too. I'd be happy to host all of you. Nothing fancy."

They all agreed.

That night, as Maura wandered through the first floor turning off lights, she couldn't help but acknowledge that time spent with friends was time well spent.

CHAPTER 23

"Either you run the day,
or the day runs you."

— Jim Rohn

Maura steered the bright red road bike onto her street. With a tap of her index and middle finger, she switched into her big chainring, clicked, and pedaled hard for the final quarter mile to her house.

Sweaty and out of breath, she leaned her bike against the garage wall and plucked the water bottle from the cage. Then she clomped over to the steps and removed her bike shoes. After taking a swig of sports drink from her bottle, she shoved her feet into her sneakers and jogged down the driveway for a one-mile run. According to Beth, she should always run after finishing a ride. The training plan suggested running a distance equal to 10 percent of the ride. Since she'd ridden ten miles, she'd run one, though she usually ran three to five. *How bad could a quick mile be?*

But no sooner had she reached the bottom of the driveway than it felt like she had lead weights attached to her ankles. Her thighs and calves tightened and cramped.

"Oh no!"

She grimaced as she belatedly recalled Beth's advice to downshift to a light gear and spin her legs for the last quarter mile of the bike ride. Something about needing to release the lactic acid buildup in the legs. Two blocks into her run, she was so uncomfortable that she walked the next block.

What have I gotten myself into?

For the remainder of her route, she ran two blocks, then walked one. By the time she entered the garage again, she understood better than ever what Dorothy meant when she said, "'There's no place like home!"

Once in the house, she recorded the ten-mile ride and torturous run in her training log. *That's a mistake I won't make twice!*

* * * * * * * * * * * * *

Maura inhaled the leftovers from last night's dinner. She had begun to notice the increase in her appetite this week. It coincided with the extra swim, bike, and run workouts she'd been doing. But despite the extra calorie burn, her face wasn't looking as gaunt as it had several weeks ago.

She had spent the morning alone and hadn't spoken to a soul all day. With the afternoon looming and no plans, she decided to head to the local library. In her last therapy session, Lydia had helped her come up with a list of places she could go where she might be around people.

After exchanging pleasantries with the librarian, Maura climbed the stairs to the second floor. It was a quiet space for reading, with comfy seating and good lighting. She nestled into a chair, opened her laptop, and worked on the career-interest inventory assigned by Lydia.

Early afternoon morphed into early evening as she completed a series of quizzes. They covered work-related skills such as time management, assertiveness, and interpersonal skills. The inventory confirmed what she already knew. Her strengths were teaching and working with her hands. She was identified as being creative with strong communication skills. Her time-management skills were top-notch, and she was a leader. As she looked over the list, an idea began to percolate.

She leaned back, rubbing her hands together as a smile spread across her face.

"You look like you just won the lottery."

"Eric! What are you doing here?" asked Maura.

"I come here all the time. It helps with my travel planning. If I haven't been to a place already, I like to research different areas so that I can plan itineraries. Call me old-school, but sometimes I like to hold a book in my hands. Plus, even if I research using my laptop, I find this a perfect workspace." His eyebrows knitted together. "What brings you here? And what were you looking so thrilled about?"

"Well, I've been seeing a therapist for the past few months. She's helping me navigate my new normal. She thinks it's time for me to focus on myself. To be honest, that's one of the reasons I agreed to do the triathlon. Anyway, she also suggested that I take a career-interest inventory." Her eyes sparkled. "I finished the inventory, and suddenly it became so clear. I want to—"

The librarian's voice sounded over the intercom. "We will be closing in ten minutes. Please finish up and exit the building."

"Can't believe I was here all afternoon. What time is it?"

"Almost five thirty," said Eric. "Hey, you can't leave me hanging! Want to head to Salsa's so you can fill me in on your plan—unless it's too personal?"

"No, I'm so excited! I have to tell someone. Let's go."

On the way, Maura recounted the morning's training debacle.

"Note to self," said Eric. "Spin legs before running!"

They sat at a high-top near the bar. Eric ordered drinks while Maura piled free buffet snacks onto plates. For the next hour, she laid out her plan for Eric.

"Do you think it's feasible?" she asked.

"I do, and the beauty is you can start slow and build at your own pace." He raised his glass. "Here's to the future."

With a clink of her glass, Maura echoed, "To the future."

* * * * * * * * * * * * * *

"That was absolutely delicious," said Stephanie as she cleared away an empty serving bowl, the solitary thin slice of onion the only remnant of Dean's homemade tuna ceviche.

"Why, thank you, Sis." Dean raised his fist, and Stephanie met him with a smile and a fist bump.

"Mom, can we see who won the DNA pool?" Sally said. "And why is it called a pool anyway?"

"Sally, stop talking," said Jake.

"All right, you two, enough," Stephanie said as she

unclipped the papers from Maura's fridge. "Sally, hand everyone their pie graph sheet. And Sam, would you mind comparing the results of everyone's graphs?"

"Why does he get to figure out the winner?" whined Sally. "This was my idea!" She crossed her arms and pursed her lips.

"Because we saved the most important job for you," Maddie said, grabbing Sally's hand. "We're going to hand out the ice cream sandwiches."

After much deliberation, no clear winner emerged, but it didn't seem to matter. For the rest of the evening, they read about the different regions identified in the results and kicked around the idea of visiting each location.

Maura stopped Dean and Stephanie as they headed for the door. "I remember that Anna asked to see these pictures of your dad." The puff of air that escaped from her nose sounded more like a bellows than a sigh.

"We're meeting her at two o'clock," added Dean. "I'll call you when we're leaving Manhattan, and we'll come straight over and tell you everything."

"I would appreciate that," said Maura, her eyes filling with tears. "I'm sorry to be so emotional."

Dean bent down and wrapped his arms around his mother. "It's okay, Mom. It's about time we come to terms with this."

* * * * * * * * * * * * * *

All morning, Maura could think of nothing but Dean and Stephanie's meeting with Anna. She welcomed the distraction of house hunting with Kara in the afternoon.

"I didn't realize this was a gated community," she said as Kara pulled up to the gatehouse at Sea Breeze adult community.

After giving their names to the security guard, they were directed to the clubhouse.

"Wow, this is quite a place," said Maura as her eyes darted from the pristine building with stately white columns to the lush landscaping skirting the perimeter.

"Who knew?" said Kara. "And we thought we would never want to live in a community like this."

They entered the lobby, where the high ceilings and shiny marble floors created a sense of sophistication. Nicole was seated in a navy wing chair next to a large fireplace with a seascape picture above the mantle.

"Hello, ladies. May I help you?" asked a tall woman in a navy button-down shirt with the Sea Breeze logo embroidered on the right breast pocket.

Nicole jumped up from her chair and waved. "Jean, these are the clients I told you about. If it's not a problem, I'd like to show them around the clubhouse."

"No problem at all, Nicole," she said, her quick smile indicating that this wasn't the first time Nicole had led a tour of the clubhouse.

"I've sold several homes in this community," Nicole said. "I really think you'll like it here, Kara." She pointed out the common room's features, which, in addition to three seating areas, housed a pool table, some high-tops, two tables for playing cards, a wet bar, and two flat-screen televisions. They made their way to the lobby.

"This is fantastic," said Kara.

"Personally, I can't wait until I'm old enough to move in here," teased Nicole. Next, they filed through the workout area, indoor pool, reading room, and conference room.

"What do you think?"

"If the house is half as nice, I'm sold. What do you think, Maura?"

"I'm speechless."

Nicole drove them to 10 Driftwood Place, a one-story single-family home. The fluffy blue hydrangeas, mint-green seagrass, and brightly colored yellow, orange, and pink portulacas complimented the beige siding and slate-blue door.

"I'll wait outside," insisted Nicole. "You two go and have a look around. When you're done, you can tell me what you think."

The women entered through a small foyer with an ample coat closet. There was a decent-sized great room. Maura could picture Kara's sectional sofa and two matching club chairs flanking the gas fireplace rather than the threadbare green-and-gold-plaid furniture filling the space at present. On the other side of the room were a glass-and-brass dining table, an open kitchen, and an island with seating for six. A four-season sunroom ran along the back of the house. Three bedrooms and two-and-a-half baths finished the floor plan.

"I love the fact that the sunroom is a space to escape to if you need privacy or don't want to watch the same TV show." A pang of loss caught her off-guard—*no need for separate spaces in her home anymore.*

"I can't wait to bring Jack back to take a look. I can see us living here, and I really think Jack will too."

"Let's head over to Josie's," said Nicole when they finished surveying the property.

As Kara drove, Maura said, "This really is a beautiful neighborhood. I may have to consider living here when I'm ready to downsize."

Nicole pulled onto Josie's driveway and parked behind Lonnie's Audi coupe.

"Come on in," Josie said when she met them at the door.

They followed her through the foyer and great room to the sunroom where Lonnie sat on a rattan tropical-print sofa, a glass of iced tea in hand. "Well, how did you make out?"

"My goodness, I love it here," Kara said. "As a matter of fact, Nicole showed us this exact model. It's amazing how the decor can make it feel so different though." Kara turned to Josie. "I love yours. The other house is a little dated."

"Nothing that paint, flooring, and a little decorating can't change," Nicole said.

"And with your sense of style, Kara, you could bring that place up to speed in no time," said Maura.

Over iced tea and fruit salad, Josie filled them in on the social dynamics of the community as well as its rules and regulations, while Nicole reviewed all of the amenities. The women even took a walk over to the clubhouse to show Lonnie.

When they returned, Kara said that Jack would be home from golfing soon and she needed to get going to fill him in on what she'd seen.

"Don't forget to call as soon as possible to schedule a time for Jack to see the house," Nicole said. "It won't last long in this market."

"Take it from someone who knows," Maura said. "If you're really serious about wanting that house, don't waste any time."

CHAPTER 24

"Morning comes whether you set the alarm or not."

– Ursula K. LeGuin

By the time Maura got home, it was almost six. She wasted no time getting to the family room. She plopped onto the sofa, her pocketbook still strapped across her chest, and stared into the distance, waiting.

Ping. The sound cut through her like a knife. The text from Stephanie read: *All went well. Can't wait to fill you in. Just through the tunnel. Be at your house in fifty minutes.*

Panic surged through Maura's body. She shot straight to the kitchen, uncorked a bottle of pinot grigio, and gave herself a healthy pour. She brought the glass to her lips and froze. She opened the fridge, placed the bottle and a full glass of wine on the top shelf, and made a cup of coffee instead. She wanted to be clearheaded when they arrived. Dinner wasn't even a thought.

She picked up her phone and scrolled through Facebook to pass the time. Better to focus on other people's situations.

One Facebook friend was sharing a picture of her lunch at a local brewpub, and another was giving an unsolicited political rant. Paul used to joke and say, "Did our trip really happen if we didn't post every meal and tourist attraction?"

Even though Maura rarely posted, she couldn't help looking at the site several times a day. She lost herself in the lives looming in front of her on the screen: this one's vacation, that one's idea of how the world should work. And then there were those adorable baby videos.

"Mom!" called Stephanie as she burst through the front door.

Maura almost tossed her phone in the air. "I'm in the kitchen," she said, her voice shaky.

Stephanie entered the room, her excitement coloring her cheeks. Dean followed, grinning. They settled in around the table.

"Where do I begin?" said Stephanie.

"At the beginning," cried Maura.

"We got to the restaurant about ten minutes late because parking was ridiculous. Anyway, the hostess led us to the back room. It was pretty crowded, but as we neared the table, we saw this woman with short dark hair." Stephanie's eyes glazed over as she stroked a piece of her long charcoal-colored hair. "Same color as mine and Dad's."

"When she saw us," Dean said, "she stood up. She was tall and thin. She looked at us and smiled."

"Mom, it was Dad's smile! We all just hugged, and it was very emotional."

Maura realized she'd been holding her breath the entire time Stephanie had been talking. She exhaled loudly. "Go on."

"We shared stories of our childhoods. Anna was an only child. Her family wasn't wealthy, but they had a nice home in upstate New York, where they moved when she was three. She made growing up in the Hudson Valley sound idyllic. We told her about life here at the Jersey Shore. She was very interested in seeing the pictures of Dad, and hearing all about you too."

"Wow!" Maura wrapped her fingers around her coffee mug. The warmth of the cup calmed her nerves. "I can understand her wanting to know about Dad, but what did she want to know about me?"

"She wanted to know if you worked, what your hobbies were, you know, just everyday stuff."

"Dean, when you located her, you said she lived in Manhattan. Are her parents still in upstate New York?"

"No, they're both deceased. Being an only child who lost her parents, she said she was thrilled when we reached out to her. She longs to connect with family."

"But here's the craziest thing," blurted Stephanie. "Toward the end of our visit, we were all getting along so well, and there was such a feeling of connection"—she paused as a look of wonder crept across her face—"I mean, you know how when you told Dad a story, he focused on you so intently that you felt like what you were saying really mattered? Like as you spoke, he'd lock eyes with you, lean forward, place an elbow on the table, and rest his chin in his hand." Stephanie mimicked each gesture, then her voice went up an octave. "Anna does the same thing!"

Maura could feel the heat rising from the base of her neck

to her forehead. "That must have been unsettling."

"Just the opposite. It made her seem so familiar. I can't explain it." She turned to Dean. "Don't you agree?"

"I do. In a weird way, it was comforting. It felt like being able to see Dad again."

"Anyway, I wandered off point. I was about to tell you the craziest thing." Stephanie inhaled deeply, closed her eyes, and shook her head quickly from side to side, like a dog expelling water from its ears after swimming.

Maura clasped the coffee mug tighter.

"So here we were bonding when all of a sudden, I'm smacked with a feeling of guilt. So I turned to her and said, 'Anna, I apologize for our Dad, and I'm so sorry he abandoned you. When Dean and I found out you existed, we were appalled that the man we idolized had walked away from you.'" A quick bark of laughter escaped from Stephanie's mouth. "Mom, you aren't going to believe this!"

"What?" asked Maura.

"Dad did take care of Anna!"

"What? What are you talking about?" She felt the color drain from her face.

"She told us she always knew she was adopted by her mother's husband—the man she called Dad. She loved him very much, and he treated her like his own. He was unfortunately killed in a car accident when Anna was twenty-five. Anyway—Mom, are you all right?"

Maura's mouth felt as if it was stuffed with cotton balls. She picked up her coffee cup, but her trembling hands forced her to set it back down.

"I'm sorry, this is just so much to digest. Go on." She tightened her grip on the mug in an attempt to hold on to reality. *Just relax and focus on what Stephanie is saying.*

"As I said, she always knew her dad wasn't her biological father. Occasionally she would ask her mother about our dad, but her mom would always say it wasn't the time to discuss it, that someday she would explain everything. So Anna grew up in a loving home and considered the man who raised her to be her dad. It wasn't until her mother got cancer last year that she began to wonder about her biological father again."

"I see," said Maura.

"She told us that right after her mother died, she went through her things and found this letter." Stephanie reached into her bag and pulled out an envelope. "She brought a copy for us. It was written by Dad!"

Maura felt light-headed. She breathed through her nose and rested her forehead in her hands as the room spun.

"Mom, are you okay?" shouted Dean as he jumped out of his chair and knelt down next to her.

Stephanie darted to the sink, grabbed a clean dishcloth, ran it under cold water, and placed it on the nape of Maura's neck.

"I'm sorry. I haven't eaten much today. I think that, combined with this coffee, has made me nauseous."

"Why don't we take off? You rest, and when you feel up to it, eat something."

Maura smiled and nodded.

"Come on, I'll help you upstairs."

Maura leaned on Dean as they climbed the stairs. He led her to the bed and helped maneuver her as she spread out on top of the comforter. Then he planted a kiss on his mother's forehead.

"Call me if you need anything," said Stephanie, who'd followed them up. She placed Maura's cell phone on the nightstand and hugged her goodbye.

Maura closed her eyes, and her head stopped spinning.

When she opened her eyes again, the room was dark. She glanced at the clock flashing nine o'clock, then sat up and turned on the bedside lamp.

Other than the sound of a car whizzing by, all she could hear was her stomach gurgling.

All right, I promised Dean I would eat.

Downstairs, Maura quickly threw together a sandwich. She filled a glass with ice and water and planted herself at the table. She bit into the soft roll with the crispy outer crust. The creamy chicken salad was just what the doctor ordered, and the ice-cold water was the perfect accompaniment. By the time she finished, she was revitalized.

She rinsed her plate, placed it in the dishwasher, and turned to exit the kitchen, but the envelope on the island caught her eye. She picked it up, knowing what was inside, yet she couldn't imagine what it said.

She returned to the fridge, retrieved the glass of wine she'd poured earlier, and sat back down. After emptying her glass, she gingerly extracted the letter and began to read.

> Dear Lisa,

Dear Lisa? Maura had assumed Paul wrote the letter to Anna. But this was written to Anna's mother. She read further.

> Dear Lisa,
>
> I am writing this letter as my wife, Maura, lies sleeping in a hospital room. This letter is my

apology; however, I'm not asking forgiveness because I am unworthy of it. Today, my wife gave birth to a son. When I held him, I couldn't stop crying. At that moment, the feeling of holding Anna for the first time came rushing back. As I stared at his face and looked into his eyes, all I could see was Anna's little face.

For the first time, I understood the enormity of deserting her. The thought of raising this child while turning my back on our child was unfathomable. It was at that moment that I knew I could no longer pretend she didn't exist.

I'm still in touch with Tommy McGill from high school. I called him earlier to tell him about my son's birth and to get your address. I know you have moved out of town, but Tommy remembered the name of the town you moved to, and that's how I was able to find your address.

Anna must be seven years old by now. I'm sure she's as pretty and smart as her mother. I also know that raising her will only get more expensive as she gets older. Music lessons, dance lessons, sports camps, not to mention college. Tomorrow I am going to open a bank account. I will name you as co-guardian and contribute to the account each month. Please use the money to help support Anna and supplement any extracurricular activities, college, etc. I will add to the account until Anna turns twenty-two. At that point, I'll assume that she's graduated from college.

I understand that I signed away my parental rights, and I don't want to get any "credit" for what I am offering. I'd prefer she never even know about this as it will only confuse her and potentially cause a rift in your family, but Lisa, please accept this support. I won't be able to live with myself otherwise.

With regrets,
Paul

Maura folded the letter carefully. She slid the paper back into the envelope. Picking up her glass, she swallowed the remaining wine, then climbed the stairs. She crawled under the covers, placed her pillow over her head, and released a gut-wrenching sob.

When she could cry no more, she flipped her pillow over, hoping the cool crisp fabric would comfort her, but it didn't.

She pushed her covers off and lay on her side, inching as far from Paul's side of the bed as possible.

"Why didn't you tell me?" she wailed into the empty space surrounding her.

Her body shook. Then she turned to Paul's side of the bed and hugged his pillow tightly. *Our lives could have been so different. We could have had a large family. We could have been more than just partners. Why weren't you honest with me?*

Like a ping-pong ball, her mood vacillated from anger to remorse. Finally, as the sun rose on the horizon, she fell into a fitful sleep.

She woke to a text at 7:00 a.m., her head throbbing. It was the first migraine she'd experienced in years, and the bright sun shining through the blinds annoyed her.

She fumbled for her glasses and read the text from Eric. *You running with us? Beth and I are at the gazebo.*

She tapped a response: *Sorry, slept through alarm. Go without me.*

She set down the phone. *What's one more lie in a life that was built around them?*

She felt like she'd been buried in a lead coffin, the crushing weight of her despair immobilizing her. The only escape was sleep, so she willed herself back into a deep slumber.

At ten, her phone woke her again. It was Stephanie. She knew she had to answer.

"Hi, Mom, how are you?"

"I'm fine. Ate and slept, and now I'm as good as new." Another lie.

"Did you get a chance to read the letter? Isn't it awesome! Dad did right by Anna. I knew he could never just pretend she didn't exist. Dean feels much better too."

Maura sat on the edge of her bed, the throbbing inside her head intensifying. "That's wonderful."

"We didn't get to tell you the best part. Dean invited Anna to his house for Father's Day. Since we'll all be there, it would be the perfect time for her to meet everyone. Anna is so excited." She giggled. "I really do get to have the sister I always wanted! Oh, gotta go. Sally and Jake are arguing. Ugh!"

Maura fell back on the bed and stared at the ceiling as her mind looped through a series of questions. *What if...? How could he...? How could I...? What if ...?*

No matter the question, no matter the answer, it was too late. She pulled the covers over her head and retreated into a deep sleep.

When she woke again, it was late afternoon. She got out of bed, headed straight to the freezer, and grabbed a pint of mint chocolate chip ice cream.

In the family room, she collapsed onto the sofa, fiddled with the remote, and stared at mindless television. When the pint of green creamy goodness was empty, she stretched out and once again fell into a sound slumber.

When she next woke, she was parched. The glow from the television cast a gloomy hue as she shuffled to the kitchen. She flicked on the light and caught a glimpse of the envelope. A visceral rage buzzed through her veins like a swarm of bees. She grabbed the envelope, tore it to shreds, and cast the pieces into the air.

"Arrrrrr!" She pressed the palms of her hands against her forehead. "Ow! My throbbing head!"

She grabbed a glass of water and two Advil and dragged herself back to her bedroom. It was as if she was caught in a nightmare and the only escape was sleep.

CHAPTER 25

"The two most powerful warriors are patience and time."

— Leo Tolstoy

The gravel underfoot, the cool breeze in her face, and the rhythmic breathing as she ran along the trail gave Maura a sense of control—something she hadn't felt since reading the letter two days ago. Often, when she needed to reason something out, she would head to the pool or jump on her bike, but today the run was the antidote.

When she'd awakened this morning, she knew she had to get out of bed. She gulped down coffee, put on shorts and a T-shirt, laced up her shoes, and headed to the park.

Halfway into the first mile, her muscles warmed up. Her stride opened and her steps grew light. Two plump bunnies scampered across the trail ahead of her, but aside from them, she had the path to herself at his early hour. She focused on nothing but her breath and her stride and was startled when she realized she'd completed the five-mile loop around the park perimeter once and was nearing the end of her sixth mile.

Back in her car, she decided she could make the eight o'clock spin class and maybe escape her mood, which seesawed between anger and despair. She pulled into the club and rummaged around for her spin shoes and bike shorts

"Yo," called Eric, from the other side of the lot, "we missed you Sunday."

Maura smiled and shrugged. She felt her insides flutter and was surprised to realize she'd missed him too. Quite a bit. She wanted to linger for a moment but knew she had to choose between talking with Eric or training. Her competitive spirit won out. "I don't want to be rude, but I've got to get inside. I went for a run, and now I'm doing an eight o'clock spin."

"Overachiever!" he shouted after her.

* * * * * * * * * * * * *

By late afternoon, Maura could no longer stave off the feeling of melancholy that had chased her all day. She made tea, grabbed a granola bar, and retreated to the sofa for another trip to TV land. One bite and one sip later, the doorbell rang.

For God's sake, go away.

She picked up the remote and began flicking channels.

Ding-dong.

Ugh! "Just a minute!" she snarled, forcing herself from the sofa and trudging to the door.

"Kara, what are you doing here?" *That was rude*. "I mean, come in."

Kara cocked an ear toward the family room and most likely heard the sad widower on TV rationalizing his hoarding addiction. Then she looked pointedly at Maura as the latter removed a piece of granola from her hair. "I wanted to return your sweater. You left it in my car on Saturday." Kara handed over a soft knit cardigan. "Are you okay? It's not like you to be inside on a beautiful afternoon watching reality TV."

"I'm fine." But before she could catch herself, a flood of tears spilled over her cheeks and down her chin, landing in plops on her tank top.

Kara wrapped her arms around her friend and rubbed her back. After a long moment, she took a step back and led Maura to the sofa. She turned off the television, headed to the kitchen, and returned with a box of tissues and two glasses of wine.

"Oh, Kara," whispered Maura before telling her everything. By the time she was done talking, a bottle of wine sat empty along with a few crumbs from one of Maura's microwaved entrees.

"Maura, you deserve a second chance. Don't forget that," said Kara as they returned to the foyer.

* * * * * * * * * * * * *

"Tell me," said Lydia, "how did the meeting with Anna and your kids go?"

Maura shook her head slowly. "You can't make this stuff up," she said and then proceeded to catch Lydia up.

"Before we address Anna, tell me how you feel about what you learned in Paul's letter."

"To be honest, I feel like I'm grieving the death of my marriage rather than just Paul, but I feel better than I did initially. It's funny, my best friend stopped by the other day.

She knew Paul and me as a couple for years. I didn't intend to, but I told her the whole story. It spilled out, and afterward, I felt so relieved. It's clear now that it all happened so long ago, and there is nothing I can do to change it. But it also made it clear how important it is to share your feelings with those close to you.

"So I've taken time over the last two days to think about what I can do differently in the future. Honest communication is an area where I've been lacking, but I plan to work on it."

"I'm sorry for what you've been going through," said Lydia, "but I'm proud of you for the way you've handled it. Now let's address your upcoming meeting with Anna. What are your concerns?"

"I know it sounds crazy, but I'm jealous of the fact that Paul had a child with someone other than me. It's why I never pushed him to reach out to her."

"That's not crazy. It's natural that meeting Paul's firstborn might make you feel insecure. No one wants to be faced with a partner's ex-lovers, let alone the child they had together. It's a reminder that you weren't Paul's one and only. It's a normal emotional response." She smiled. "You do know intellectually that Anna is not a threat."

"You're right," said Maura. "I was so convinced that Anna was going to be resentful or hurtful toward Dean and Stephanie, but according to them, she's neither."

"Approach your meeting with an open heart and mind. You owe it to both yourself and Paul."

Maura's eyes filled quickly, but tears did not spill over.

* * * * * * * * * * * * *

Later that afternoon as Maura set the table, a warm breeze moved across the porch, leaving behind the slightest scent of honeysuckle. It always reminded her of the perfume she wore in high school. She laughed to herself. Back then she knew exactly how she wanted the future to look. She never could have predicted any of this. Then a John Lennon lyric popped into her head: "Life is what happens to you while you're busy making other plans."

It wasn't long before the supper club ladies were lounging on the wicker set, drinks in hand, chatting away.

"I have some news!" squealed Kara during a rare lull.

As Kara spoke, Nicole broke into an ear-to-ear grin.

"We have a contract on our house," Kara continued, "and we made an offer on the one in Josie's community."

"That's fantastic!" said Josie.

"I told you this is a hot market," said Nicole.

"You're going to love low-maintenance living," added Lonnie. She looked at Maura. "No offense."

"None taken," said Maura. "I must admit, seeing Sea Breeze and its amenities did plant a seed."

"Just let me know when you're ready," said Nicole with a lilt in her voice.

"I hear a timer going off in the kitchen," said Lonnie.

"Instead of reheating," Maura said, "I decided to cook tonight. Why don't you refill your glasses while I bring out the food?"

"I'll help," said Kara.

In the kitchen, Kara slid her arm around Maura's shoulders. "How are you? You seem much more settled."

"I am. After confiding in you and talking with Lydia, I feel much better."

"I'm so glad to hear that. I was worried about you."

"Thank you, friend," said Maura as she turned and gave Kara a bear hug. "But I'm okay. Now, let's get this dinner out to the porch before I get emotional."

The women feasted on Caprese salad, crusty Italian bread, and homemade eggplant parmigiana.

"Once again, this meal is outstanding," said Kara as she waved a piece of bread in the air for effect.

"The eggplant is so light. How did you do it?" asked Lonnie.

"Years ago, Paul came up with the idea of slicing the eggplant thin, drizzling a little olive oil, and grilling it rather than frying. When I assemble the layers, I just sprinkle seasoned whole wheat bread crumbs, tomato sauce, and freshly grated mozzarella cheese on top. It alleviates the heavy, oily element."

"You should open a cooking school," joked Nicole. "Maura's Magnificent Meals."

Everyone at the table nodded in agreement.

"It's funny you say that because that's exactly what I intend to do," said Maura.

"Are you serious?" asked Nicole "That's an awesome idea!"

"Tell us about it," said Josie

Maura explained that her idea was to start small and work out of her own kitchen. She envisioned offering couples' classes, children's parties, and girls'-night-out experiences.

"I'm just in the idea stage at the moment, but I feel like it's feasible. When Paul and I put in this industrial kitchen, I never imagined I'd use it that way, but then again, I never imagined any of this." She raised her glass. "To the future!"

“To the future!” they responded, clinking glasses.

Over Lonnie’s low-calorie pineapple-cheesecake bars, Nicole seemed to cautiously work up the nerve to ask a question. “So, Maura, I hope you don’t mind me asking, but how did the kids’ meeting with Anna go? When you didn’t bring it up in the locker room, I assumed you were waiting until tonight to tell us about it.”

Kara shot a wide-eyed look at Maura, who answered calmly. “Surprisingly well. They were all delighted to meet and got along famously. In fact, Dean invited Anna to his house for a Father’s Day celebration on Sunday.”

“I’m glad it went so well,” Josie said. “But how do you feel about meeting her so soon?”

“You know, I wasted so much energy anticipating the worst, but all went well, so I’ve decided to relax and be open to a positive relationship.”

“That’s a good course of action,” said Josie.

Maura rose from her chair and gestured for everyone to come close. “Group hug,” she cried. They stood for a moment with their arms linked, and the bond, at least to Maura, felt tangible.

Lying in bed that night, she was overwhelmed with a feeling of gratitude for the women who had come out of the locker room and into her life.

CHAPTER 26

"The best time to plant a tree is twenty years ago. The second best time is now."

— *Unknown*

"I'm going to be sore tomorrow," said Eric as he, Beth, and Maura filed out of the exercise studio.

The women nodded their heads in agreement.

"How does Saturday sound for a brick?" asked Beth.

"A what?" asked Eric.

"A brick," repeated Beth. "Brick workouts train your body to handle the demands of shifting from one muscle group to another. It's really important when training for a triathlon to stack two legs of the event back-to-back. Think of it as a stack of bricks, although some people call it a brick because after completing a ride and a run, your legs feel like bricks."

Beth looked at Maura and Eric's panicked expressions. "Don't worry, you've got this," she assured them. "We'll begin with an eight-mile ride at the park, followed by a one-mile run after."

Maura glanced at Eric. He looked excited, but she felt only apprehension.

"I attempted a brick last week and it was torture," said Maura. "I forgot to spin out my legs, and my run was miserable. My legs felt like lead weights."

Beth giggled. "That's one newbie mistake you won't make twice!"

They agreed to meet at 7:00 a.m. on Saturday at the park's north lot.

"I've got to go," Beth said. "Don't forget to bring riding gear and running shoes." She dashed to the gym exit.

Maura and Eric turned toward the locker rooms.

"Hey," said Eric, "there's a Bollywood movie showing at The Art House. Want to join me tonight for dinner and a movie?"

"I'd love to."

"I'll meet you at the theater at six. Any preference for dinner?"

Maura's face lit up. "How about a theme night? We'll grab Indian food. I've been dying to try that new restaurant."

"I never met a curry I didn't like. I'll see you at six."

* * * * * * * * * * * * *

The dining room floors were sleek gold-and-brown marble. Mid-century-style tables and chairs, made of blond wood, were checkered throughout the room. It could be any trendy restaurant serving inventive cuisine, except for the soft sitar music and the fact that all of the food servers were South

Asian males. Their thin-lapel black suits and crisp white button-down shirts, open at the collar, lent an air of sophistication, not unlike the menu. The kitchen was open to the dining area, and a handful of patrons sat at counter seats and watched the cooks orchestrate the meals.

Maura and Eric sat in the front of the restaurant next to the window. The setting sun painted the sky a purplish pink, enhancing the ambiance of the room.

Eric leaned forward in his chair and whispered, "I hope the food is as good as the vibe."

"The waiters look like they're ready for an *Esquire* photoshoot," said Maura.

"That's the look you like? I'll keep it in mind."

"Hmm, and what look do you like?" said Maura, surprised at her flirtatious response.

"I like petite women with simple, classic style."

Maura looked down at her aqua button-down and khaki skirt. When she looked up, she was met with Eric's playful wink and could feel her face flushing. In an attempt to deflect his attention, she threw her napkin across the table.

With an effortless swoop, Eric caught it in his hand. "Hey, what was that for? You asked." He chuckled as he returned the crisp white swatch to Maura.

With some direction from their waiter, they decided on a spicy lamb entrée and a smoky chicken dish.

"What did you think of the movie?" asked Maura between mouthfuls of the avocado, puffed rice, and chutney appetizer they were sharing.

"I could take or leave the story, but that scenery made me want to go on a trek to the mountains of north India."

"The cinematography blew me away."

"Talk about being blown away, this food is amazing," said Eric.

The waiter delivered the entrees. The savory flavors of Maura's dish, along with its hint of cardamom, warmed her insides, while her growing friendship with Eric warmed her heart.

"I'm surprised that with all of your travels, you've never been to India," she said.

Eric's smile stretched from ear to ear. "Funny you should say that."

Maura cocked her head, and Eric explained. "My parents both passed, but after my father retired, he was… how shall I say? He was at sea. He ran a small family-style restaurant, where the hours were long, and he rarely missed a day's work. When he finally decided to sell the business, my mother was thrilled. She thought my dad would finally take some time for himself and relax; instead, he drove her crazy. After a year, she called me and asked if I could give him a job at my travel agency. I thought it was a great idea. He came to work three days a week, filed paperwork, answered the phone, and greeted customers. One day over lunch, I told him that I was planning a trip to India, so I shared my itinerary. He had no interest in going, but he asked if he could book my flights. Of course, I agreed.

"Several weeks later, my departure date arrived. I stopped by the office to tie up loose ends before leaving, and he handed me a folder with my itinerary and plane tickets. At the airport, I checked my bags and headed to the gate, totally preoccupied because it was the first time I was leaving my business in someone else's hands. So I boarded the plane, took a sleeping pill, and immediately fell to sleep. It felt like only minutes had passed before I awoke to a flight attendant shaking my shoulder and saying we were about to land. You can imagine my surprise when the pilot announced the time and temperature in Delhi, Delaware!"

They both burst into laughter and were just gathering themselves when the waiter approached.

"Can I interest you in dessert?" he said.

"Oh, no thank you," replied Maura, catching her breath as she dabbed her eyes with a napkin. "But as you can see by our empty plates, the food was scrumptious."

"We'll just take the check," said Eric, smiling.

A few moments later the waiter returned with a small plate and two forks. "Compliments of the chef." He set down two sweet-cheese dumplings with pear custard, garnished with a sprig of fresh rosemary. "Sometimes when Chef sees a happy couple enjoying the food and each other, he gifts them a sweet. Guests like the two of you are the reason we do what we do. Delivering happiness through innovative cuisine." He bowed with clasped hands and nodded at the pair. "Enjoy."

Maura looked at Eric with an uneasy grin and shrugged.

He smiled and turned to the waiter. "Please tell Chef we are honored."

"This tastes like heaven," said Maura, plunging her fork in for another bite. "But I feel guilty. He thinks we're a couple!"

"We wouldn't want to insult him."

"You're right, it would be bad karma!" agreed Maura with a smirk as she steered her fork back to the dumpling.

* * * * * * * * * * * * *

Maura sat up in bed on Sunday morning. Tossing the rumpled

bed sheet aside, she swung her legs to the floor, took two steps toward the bathroom, and stopped in her tracks. Her lower back felt like someone had snuck into her bedroom in the middle of the night and clamped her spine in a vice. She caught a glimpse of herself in the cheval glass. *I look more like a hunchback than a triathlete.* She winced as she forced herself to stand up straight. Yesterday's bike ride had taken its toll.

Returning from the bathroom, she texted Eric and Beth: *Why are we doing this triathlon?*

Eric shot back a response: *Because we can!*

Beth immediately "liked" his comment.

Maura giggled and tapped: *Thanks for reminding me*, followed by a smiley face emoji.

* * * * * * * * * * * * *

Unlike Mother's Day, Father's Day was a testosterone-fest with the men grilling meat, drinking beer, and talking trash while playing Wiffle ball in Dean and Maddie's backyard. It was up to the remaining family members to do what they could to assist, which usually meant keeping the cooler stocked.

Maura couldn't help but notice a shiny white SUV with New York plates parked along the curb as she pulled up to Dean's house. *Deep, slow breaths*, she reminded herself as the familiar knot in her stomach began to grow.

"Gran!"

Now in the driveway, Maura was startled by Sally, whose cherubic face beamed on the other side of the window.

"Come inside and meet Auntie Anna. Isn't that funny? Her

name makes me think of the pretzels we get at the mall!"

Maura smiled as she got out of her car, but her breath quickened, and her mind raced.

"Hurry up, Gran!" said Sally, darting toward the backyard.

Cheers and playful groans echoed from the Wiffle-ball field as Maura entered the yard. "I'll be right back," she said. "I need the ladies' room." Without waiting for a reply, she pulled her hand free of Sally's grasp and ran to the powder room off the kitchen. She shut and locked the door behind her. Then she promptly threw up.

When she stood, she stared at her reflection in the mirror. *Get yourself together!*

Maura rinsed her mouth and blotted her face with a damp washcloth. For a fleeting moment, she thought about running out the front door, jumping into her car, and rushing home to bed, but she had no choice. It was time to face Paul's past and her present.

She ran her fingers through her hair, straightened her clothes, and plastered a smile on her face before exiting.

"Happy Father's Day!" she exclaimed as she stepped onto the deck.

Dean turned from the grill. "Thanks, Mom!" He spread his arms for a hug.

"Hey, what about me?" said Kyle, approaching with two beers in hand. He tossed one to Dean.

"Mom," called Stephanie, "I thought you'd never get here!"

Maura turned toward Stephanie, then scanned the yard. "Where's Anna?" But she was relieved when she didn't see a new face anywhere.

"She ran to her car to grab sunglasses. I can't wait for you to meet her." Stephanie looked past Maura and gestured to someone. "Here she is! Anna, come meet my mom."

Maura turned to see a tall, thin woman with a short dark bob. Her black-and-white polka dot sundress and stylish red leather tote were as chic as her designer sunglasses. Anna extended a hand while simultaneously pinching the arm of her sunglasses. She slid them to the crown of her head to expose eyes so similar to Paul's that Maura gasped involuntarily. But she rebounded and forced a smile while extending her hand.

"I'm so happy to meet you," said Anna.

Maura felt thrown when Anna cleared her throat—just like Paul used to do when he was nervous.

"Okay, everyone," Dean called. "Come and get it!"

"Come on, Auntie Anna," yelled Sally as she grabbed Anna's hand. "Sit next to me."

The teak dining table was laden with a platter of sliced London broil, juicy and pink. A second platter boasted grilled sausages with vertical marks striping the crispy casings. A bowl of roasted potatoes and a robust pasta salad rounded out the meal.

Plates were piled high, and seats were selected. Sam then stood, tapping his knife against the side of his glass.

"In honor of Father's Day, Jake, Sally, and I have written a poem."

"It was my idea," Sally said. "We made an acoustic poem from the word FATHER. My teacher showed us how to do it."

"Nobody cares, Sally, and it's an *acrostic* poem, not acoustic," Jake said.

"Without further ado," announced Sam, turning to Sally.

Sally stood with her shoulders back and chest forward. "Father, F is for Fun."

They took turns reading the poem.

Jake was next. " A is for Awesome," he said as he leaned across his mother to fist-bump Kyle.

Zeroing in on Dean, Sam said. "T is for Thoughtful."

It was Sally's turn again. "H is for Handsome," she declared, and she blew Kyle a kiss.

"Oohs" and "ahhs" echoed through the yard.

"E is for Encouraging," said Jake.

"Father, R is for Rad," declared Sam with a smile as he raised his hand, extended his thumb and pinky, and rotated his wrist.

Everyone clapped as the children bowed.

Over dinner, Maura listened as Anna was bombarded with a barrage of questions.

"Dad said you live in New York City. Do you like it?" asked Sam.

"I love it! I grew up in a small town in Upstate New York. It was pretty quiet—that is unless it was tourist season. Then it was bustling. I loved the excitement the crowds would bring, so at a fairly young age, I decided that when I grew up, I wanted to live in a city. And what better city than New York City?"

Maura sighed with relief. *Sounds like she got what she wanted. At least she won't be comparing herself to Dean and Steph.*

"Do you have a job?" asked Sally.

"Mm-hmm," she replied. "I went to college and majored in journalism." At Sally's confused expression, she clarified. "Writing."

"Oh, I love to write," said Sally.

Maura smiled inside. *College education, check.*

"I'm not surprised," Anna said. "Your poem rocked."

Sally beamed.

"Anyway, I worked at a small newspaper back home for a little while, but I wasn't happy. Like I told Sam, I grew up in a tourist spot, and from the time I was fourteen, I worked in restaurants and loved it." She addressed the table. "After some soul-searching, I quit my job and went back to school, this time to culinary school. Then I graduated, moved to Manhattan, and worked in a bunch of kitchens. Fast forward to today, I've combined my love of writing and restaurants." She grinned ear to ear. "I'm a blogger. I review New York City restaurants."

Stephanie couldn't contain herself. "I read your blog all the time!" She laughed. "I picked the restaurant where we met based on your blog! I never imagined that the Anna Anderson we were meeting for lunch was the Anna Anderson who reviewed the restaurant."

Everyone at the table burst into laughter at the irony.

As the cackles died down, Sally let out one last giggle and then blurted, "What are we laughing at anyway?" which sent everyone back into hysterics again.

"That meal was wonderful," said Anna, clearing the table.

Stephanie snatched the plate from her hands. "Why don't you and Mom sit and chat while we clean up?" She gestured toward the seating area, where two empty wine glasses awaited. "Get to know each other."

Maura and Anna settled onto a sofa on the far side of the deck. Anna filled their wine glasses and took a sip before setting her glass on the table. Maura held hers, running her fingers up and down the long thin stem. After an awkward moment, Maura broke the silence. "You know, I was concerned when Dean and Stephanie told me they were meeting you." She saw a look of worry flash across Anna's face. "But they are so excited they found you." She gestured to the crowd. "Everyone is." She smiled at Anna.

"Your family is amazing. I didn't think I would feel connected so quickly. But this must be strange for you."

"Honestly, I thought it would be." Emboldened by the wine, she took Anna's hands in her own and peered into her eyes. "But connecting with you is like connecting with a piece of Paul." She sighed. "I'm sorry you didn't have a chance to get to know him."

"I can't say I never wondered about what he was like or why he wasn't in my life, but I can assure you that my parents loved me. They supported me in every way possible. I wish Paul could have gotten to know my Dad. He had a huge impact on the person I am today. Ever since I found Paul's letter, I've been so curious to meet all of you. I used to dream of having siblings, and when my parents passed, I felt like an orphan. When Dean and Stephanie reached out, it was like being given a second chance at a family." Anna's eyes glistened.

Maura was overcome with profound sadness. "I'm so thankful now that we've all met. I think I speak for all of us when I say, Welcome to the family!"

"Gran," Sally shouted as she ran over, "it's time for dessert!" She leaned between them and stage-whispered, "Mom bought an ice cream cake that looks like a necktie! She's about to bring it out and surprise the dads!"

With the family gathered around the table again, Anna asked the grandkids about favorite sports, subjects, and hobbies until the cake had been devoured and the children had run off to play flashlight tag.

Conversation flowed as easily as the summer breeze, which tickled the wind chimes that hung from the old oak adjacent to the deck. They shared stories—some funny, some heartwarming—and new familial bonds seemed to form. By the end of the evening, they made plans for the next get-together.

"So it's settled," said Maura. "Anna, you'll join us at my house on the Fourth of July. Plan to spend the night. I have more than enough room."

"That sounds great," Anna said with excitement in her voice. "I can't wait!"

Sally ran by and waved her flashlight at the table. "Come and play tag with us, Aunt Anna."

Sally disappeared in a flash, like the glint of light that bounced off the sliver of metal peeking out of the red leather tote bag at Anna's feet.

CHAPTER 27

Sobremesa (Spanish): When the food has finished but the conversation is still flowing.

* * * * * * * * * * * * *

Maura arrived at Salsa and found Lonnie talking to the hostess.

"I'm getting us a table," she explained. "The bar is too crowded and noisy. We'll still get happy hour prices for our drinks; we just can't eat from the buffet."

"I'm sure no one will mind," said Maura.

Soon they were gathered around a table. Orders had been placed, and drinks had been delivered. It was time for Maura to fill them in on yesterday's visit with Anna. When she was done, Kara reached across the table and squeezed Maura's hand. "I'm so glad it all worked out."

"Me too. I was convinced something was going to go

wrong. I just kept thinking that she might want to get back at Dean and Steph for growing up with the father she never knew." She took a sip of her margarita. "I'm so relieved I was wrong. She even said that she wished Paul could have met her stepdad so he could have seen how well she was taken care of."

Josie pressed her hand to her heart. "I'm so happy for all of you."

"So, what's next?" asked Lonnie.

"Believe it or not, she's coming to my house for the Fourth. I even invited her to spend the night. It's such a contradiction. Anna seems like both stranger and family at the same time." Maura rested her forearms on the table, laced her fingers together, and leaned forward. "Did I mention she has Paul's eyes? And Dean and Stephanie commented that she has his smile. There is something so familiar about her. Some of her mannerisms even mimic Paul's."

"That's creepy," said Nicole. "But in a cool way."

Maura nodded her head in agreement. "You can't run from DNA."

"Isn't that your friend Eric over there?" asked Lonnie as she gestured toward a table in the back of the restaurant.

Maura grinned as her mind flashed back to dinner at the Indian restaurant. She turned to see Eric lean in and let out a belly laugh as his female companion pointed to something on her phone screen. The smile faded from Maura's face as she inhaled sharply and realized the uneasy feeling in her stomach was a pang of jealousy.

"I hate to drink and dash, but I'm meeting Harris for a quick drink at eight," explained Nicole. "I'll fill you all in on Wednesday. Maura, are we still on for Wednesday dinner?"

"Absolutely!" Pushing Eric and his date out of her mind, she continued in a more controlled tone. "If I miss you at the club, I'll see you Wednesday night."

As she crawled into bed that night, her thoughts spun like the ceiling fan above her.

* * * * * * * * * * * * *

At supper club, the women sat at Maura's table long after the plates had been cleared away. Even though they'd just had dinner together a few nights ago, the chatter rarely stopped.

"Okay, Nicole," said Maura, "how about those Harris updates?"

Nicole got up to fill the empty water pitcher while the women awaited her response. She returned to the table, refilled her glass, and asked, "Would anyone else like some water?"

"Nicole," cried Lonnie, "get to the point or you're going to be wearing that water!"

Nicole set the pitcher on the table, smoothed her skirt, and began. "Okay, the other night at the bar, Harris invited me to his brother's house for a Fourth of July party, and I'm pretty sure there's going to be fireworks that night." She snickered as she raised her hand, snapped her fingers three times, and whipped her head back. "If you know what I mean."

They all howled with laughter.

"So much for taking it slow," teased Kara.

"Excuse me?" said Lonnie. "For Nicole, this is moving slower than the Great Molasses Flood of 1919."

"I can't dispute what I don't know. What was the Great Molasses Flood of 1919?" asked Nicole, her eyebrows rising.

"In Boston, a tank of molasses burst and released 2.3 million gallons of sticky syrup into the streets. It was devastating. Twenty-one people died!"

"Oh yeah, I'm going to die if Harris doesn't make a move soon!"

Laughter echoed through the house.

"You outdid yourself once again," called Josie as the women made their way down the driveway to their cars.

"You're too kind," shouted Maura from the front porch as she waved goodbye to her dear friends.

* * * * * * * * * * * * *

Friday morning's core class was as challenging as ever. Maura wiped the sweat from her forehead, picked up her medicine ball, and walked to the back of the exercise studio. She placed her ball in the storage bin, turned, and bumped into Eric.

"Oh my gosh! I'm so sorry. I wasn't paying attention," she said as pins and needles pierced her cheeks.

"Hey, no worries." Noticing the pink blush of her cheeks, he repeated. "Really, no big deal."

After an awkward moment of silence, Eric asked, "Are you done working out for the day?"

"I'm going to run three miles."

"Mind if I join you?"

Why don't you run with your Salsa chickie? "Sure, meet in the lobby in five."

They headed for a nearby bike path and ran in silence for the first five minutes.

"You're awfully quiet this morning," said Eric.

"I guess I just don't have much to say."

"Did I ever tell you about the time my friends coaxed me into a five-mile beer run? A local bar sponsored the race. If you had a race number, you got to drink for free until noon. I wasn't in shape, but it sounded like a good time. By the end of the first mile, I was struggling, and my friends had left me in the dust. I knew it would take me forever to finish, so I cut through some yards and made my way to the bar. By the time they showed up, I was two beers in, and they couldn't figure out how I beat them!" He burst into a self-deprecating laugh.

Maura couldn't help herself. She laughed along with him. "Did you ever tell them the truth?"

"As a matter of fact, I did, the last time we all got together. I figured ten years had passed, so the statute of limitations on being disqualified had probably expired."

Maura gestured to a bench. "Can we sit for a moment? I need to talk to you."

"Of course." Eric sat down next to her, wiping sweat from his forehead.

"Ugh! I feel like a confused teenager, but I want to be honest with you." She crossed her arms and legs. "I've made a promise to myself to communicate better. Someday I'll tell you all about how I learned that lesson, but that's another story." She tucked her foot behind her bottom leg and tightened the clasp of her folded arms. "On Monday night, I was at Salsa having dinner with the girls, and before I left, I saw you at a table in the back—with a woman. You were looking at her phone and laughing." Beads of sweat formed on her forehead. "I'm so embarrassed to say this, but I felt jealous. I know I'm vulnerable right now, but I feel like I have a crush on you." She sat tall and looked him in the eye.

"Wow!"

"I'm sorry. I can't believe I just said that. I feel so stupid! I'm sorry if I made you uncomfortable." Tears welled up. She closed her eyes and tilted her head to the sky. *Control yourself, Maura.*

"Maura," Eric said softly. "Maura, look at me."

She turned to him as he gently grasped her hands in his.

"First of all, I saw you on Monday night too. I walked by your table and was going to say hello, but you were talking to your friends so intensely. They were hanging on your every word." Eric shrugged. "I didn't want to interrupt. Secondly, I was with my friend Ben's wife. We were waiting for him to meet us. Actually, Ben was one of the guys who talked me into signing up for that race I just told you about. Anyway, while we were waiting, Ben's wife showed me a video of their baby tasting a lemon for the first time!" He laughed. "I don't know why you would do that to your kid, let alone tape it, but his expression was priceless!"

Maura tilted her head and smiled.

Eric continued. "And, third—now listen to me carefully." He squeezed her hands. "I don't have a crush on you."

Her stomach dropped. She closed her eyes and wished she could vanish into thin air.

Eric squeezed her hands again. "Look at me," he pleaded.

Her eyes felt as if they were glued shut.

"Maura, please."

She slowly opened her eyes. Warmth emanated from his gaze. "I don't have a crush on you; I'm falling in love with you." He smiled, and the crow's feet around his eyes deepened.

Did he just say, love?

"I agree that you're vulnerable right now," he continued,

"and I don't want to take advantage of that, because you mean more to me than any woman has for a very long time."

Her thoughts spun wildly. It had been a long while since a man had stirred such emotion within her. It excited and terrified her at the same time.

"Eric—"

"Maura, I've thought a lot about this, and I want to move very slowly. It's only fair to you and your family."

Unable to speak, she nodded in agreement.

"I want to ask you out on a date. Next April, I'd love to take you to Washington, D.C., to see the cherry blossoms."

She surprised herself with a laugh. "I've always wanted to do that!"

"Then it's a date." Eric chuckled. "Mark that on your calendar. Now come on, we have a triathlon to train for. Let's sprint telephone poles!"

CHAPTER 28

"'Cause a little bit of summer's
what the whole year is about."

— John Mayer

"Welcome!" exclaimed Maura as she greeted Anna in the driveway. "Come on in, and I'll show you to your room." She gave Anna a hug and then led her toward the house. "I could have picked you up at the train station, you know."

"That's okay. I don't mind taking Ubers. Wow!" Anna gasped as she eyed the Persian area rug and antique grandfather clock adorning the foyer. "Your home is more beautiful than I imagined."

"Thank you, you're too kind." Maura gestured toward the stairs. "Your room is the second door on the left. Why don't you freshen up? The party doesn't start for a few hours. I'll give you the ten-cent tour when you come back down."

"That sounds great," said Anna, carrying her red leather

tote and canvas duffle up the stairs.

"I'll be in the kitchen if you need me."

Maura placed a baking dish of creamy macaroni and cheese into the oven and set the timer. Her cutting board and knife block were at the ready on the island. After slicing a pineapple and avocado, she set a portion aside and chopped the remainder for a Mexican salad.

It was the Fourth of July, and she planned to serve traditional fare with a twist: grilled hot dogs and hamburgers with an array of toppings, grilled pineapple, avocado, tater tots, mac and cheese, grilled poblanos, caramelized onion, bacon, and a platter of over-easy eggs.

She rinsed the black beans and dumped them in a bowl, added chopped onion, peppers, cilantro, and the chopped avocado and pineapple. Then she drizzled some olive oil and added a generous squeeze of lime. She covered the bowl with plastic wrap and set it in the fridge. After grabbing the bacon and eggs, she pushed the refrigerator door shut with her knee and turned to find Anna just inches away.

She yelped. The bacon and eggs hit the floor with a thud. Egg yolks tumbled from the carton onto the tile floor and splashed her sandal, while the thick yellow liquid seeped between her toes. "Oh, you startled me!"

"I didn't mean to frighten you," said Anna calmly.

"It's okay," Maura assured her. "I'll just ask Stephanie to pick up more eggs on her way over." She dabbed a paper towel between her toes. "Excuse me for just a minute. I'm going to run upstairs and change my sandals."

She returned to the kitchen to find Anna standing by the sink and staring out the window.

"I hope you remembered your bathing suit," said Maura.

"Actually, I don't have one. You know, city life." She shrugged. "I don't even know how to swim. Never learned." A tinge of coolness had entered her voice.

Maura felt her cheeks flush. "Oh, I just assumed—"

"Hi, Gran. Hi, Aunt Anna," called Sam as he entered the kitchen. Dean and Maddie were just a few steps behind.

Dean greeted Maura with a hug and a kiss on the cheek. "Here I am, at your service." He turned to Anna. "It's great to see you again."

"It's great to be here. Hi, Maddie." The earlier coolness had been replaced with warmth.

Everyone got to work. Dean and Sam worked in the backyard, while Maddie set up the porch, and Anna worked alongside Maura in the kitchen.

"You clearly know your way around a kitchen," said Maura. "Your knife skills are amazing."

Anna stopped chopping and held up the knife, swinging it back and forth as if she were waving a flag. "Culinary school and countless kitchen jobs give a girl excellent cutting technique."

She steeled her gaze on Maura, her expression stoic, but a grin crept across her face as Stephanie entered with the eggs.

By five o'clock, the party was jumping. Small flags had been planted in the flowering pots. A flag bunting had been draped across the outside of the screen porch, and Jimmy Buffett was singing about cheeseburgers.

When the meal was ready, Anna built her hot dog, loading it with grilled pineapple, avocado, and bacon. She dipped the serving spoon into the mac and cheese and plopped a mound of creamy noodles onto her plate.

"What an idyllic childhood it must have been here," she

said in a dreamy voice to no one in particular.

"Oh, it was wonderful," said Stephanie, dumping caramelized onions onto her burger. "We still love coming here."

Maura smiled and sighed, ignoring the dark clouds rolling in from the west. "Even without Paul here, I think we've been pretty successful today."

In the distance, a clap of thunder erupted with a boom. It suddenly became dark, and a lightning bolt streaked across the sky. Within moments, cold plops of rain drenched the yard, and a gusting wind soaked the porch.

"Grab something and get inside," said Maura.

In a flash, everyone jumped into action. Dinners, drinks, platters, and bowls were scooped up. It wasn't long before they were all gathered around Maura's kitchen table as if nothing had happened.

"My goodness," said Anna, "you all handled that like a fine-tuned machine."

Dean piped up. "Trust me, there have been countless times that we've had a yard full of people basking in the sun one minute, then charging to the porch the next." He turned to Stephanie. "Remember the pool party for my tenth birthday?"

Stephanie laughed. "You mean your Olympic birthday party?"

"Mom made a cake with the Olympic rings on it," Dean said. "And Dad had us compete in all those crazy races. One minute it was sunny and hot, the next it was teeming rain."

"You and your friends were supposed to sleep outside in a tent," Maura said, "but ended up sprawled throughout the family room. I found candy and crumbs between my sofa cushions for weeks afterward."

"And what was better as a kid than sitting on the screened porch with a book while the rain poured down outside?" said Stephanie. She inhaled slowly as if sniffing a bouquet. "The air was musky yet sweet. I still love that smell."

"Dad, how come you never had an Olympic birthday party for me?" asked Sam, his brow furrowing.

"Your birthday is in February!"

"Haven't you heard of the Winter Olympics?"

"Speaking of sports," said Stephanie to Anna, "did Mom tell you that she's training for a triathlon?"

"Wow, that's impressive."

"Well," Maura said, her cheeks turning pink, "it's only a sprint."

"Only a sprint means that she will swim a quarter mile in the ocean, then get on her bike and ride twelve miles, and finish with a three-mile run!" explained Dean.

"Actually, it is a 3.1-mile run, but who's counting?" Maura whipped her neck, tossing her hair over her shoulder. "Seriously though, I just hope I'm ready. I have until the end of the summer to train." She glanced at Anna. "As a matter of fact, I'm going on a ride tomorrow morning, but it won't interfere with getting you to the station at eleven fifteen."

"Don't worry about me," Anna said.

"Hey, I have an idea," said Jake. "Since it's raining, why don't we watch some old DVDs of when Mom and Uncle Dean were kids?"

Stephanie turned to Anna. "Would you like that? You could get a look at Dad in action."

Anna swallowed the last gulp of her beer before answering. "There's nothing I'd like more."

* * * * * * * * * * * * *

Sam eased the last DVD out of the player and placed it back in its case.

"Thanks for sharing your memories with me," Anna said. "Those DVDs are priceless."

She stood and raised her arms above her head, fingertips reaching toward the ceiling, and let out a big yawn. "Oh, excuse me. It's been a long day." She smiled at the group. "But don't get me wrong. I've enjoyed every minute." She took a step toward the kitchen. "I'm going to grab a glass of water. Can I get anyone anything?"

Sally cupped her hands around Stephanie's ear, then skipped over to Maura and wrapped her arms around her waist. "Mom said if it's okay with you, I can spend the night." She squeezed her grandmother tighter. "Can I? Please!"

"Of course, honey. Anna's staying in your mom's old room, so you'll stay in Uncle Dean's room tonight."

"She has a softball game tomorrow," Stephanie said, "so I'll pick her up at eight."

"No problem," said Maura. "I'll have her up early and ready to go." She turned to Sam. "Sam, would you mind putting these DVDs back in the spare room closet?"

"Sure, Gran," he said as he picked up the old wine carton, now used to store the DVDs, and sprinted up the stairs.

"I'm going to tell Aunt Anna I'm staying over!" Sally announced as she ran to the kitchen.

"Mom, when are you going to get rid of that old DVD player and let me convert those discs to a cloud storage format?" asked Dean.

"I don't know. I hate learning new technology."

"I know, but you don't even know how to hook up the DVD player by yourself. Why not let us show you how to stream? It's much easier."

"I'll think about it," Maura said, slightly exasperated at the thought of yet another change.

When they'd all assembled back in the family room, they said their goodbyes.

Stephanie stepped toward Anna and gave her a hug. "We will have to get together again soon."

Maura, Anna, and Sally waved from the front porch as they watched the cars roll down the street.

"Well, ladies," said Maura as she shut and locked the front door. "Are you ready to call it a night?"

"I certainly am," said Anna.

"Oh, okay," whined Sally before flashing a grin. "Last one upstairs is a rotten egg!" She dashed up the stairs.

CHAPTER 29

"Life is too short for long-term grudges."

— Elon Musk

"Anna," said Maura as Sally bounded up the steps, "I'm going to grab a glass of water to bring upstairs. Would you like one?"

"Yes, thanks."

Maura walked to the kitchen while Anna remained in the foyer, taking in her surroundings. She glanced into the dining room, the streetlight bouncing off the highly polished Queen Anne dining table and ornate chandelier with its Austrian crystals twinkling. She turned to peruse the formal living room: pale walls, creamy upholstery, and fireplace mantle littered with family photos. She wandered back to the kitchen, her eyes scanning the industrial appliances and the large clunky farm table, its distressed wood contrasting with the sleek finish of the marble countertops.

Anna peered into the family room, where they had gathered

to watch the Antonelli family memories, each DVD opening a window into the life she never lived. The same family room where she'd seen and heard Paul, her biological father, for the first time that she could remember. She was struck by the similarities shared between the two of them. His hair, his eyes, his height—all traits she had inherited.

How appropriate, she thought, to watch movies of the family she had never been part of—in their *family* room.

Her heart raced as her fingernails dug into her palms.

"Calm down," she muttered to herself.

Maura returned with a small pitcher of water, the lid doubling as a glass. "Here, take this."

Anna relaxed her hands and reached for the carafe. She ran her free hand over the smooth, bulbous newel post at the base of the railing and lingered at the bottom of the stairs.

I wonder if Dean or Stephanie ever slid down this banister when they were young. She clenched her teeth to maintain her composure. Then she climbed the stairs slowly, rehearsing tomorrow's plan.

She entered the bedroom and sat on the edge of Stephanie's old bed. The cotton-candy-pink walls and white furniture made her feel nauseous.

She set the carafe next to a trophy with a ponytailed girl rearing her head back to make contact with a soccer ball. She leaned forward to take a closer look and nearly fell off the bed when Sally popped up from underneath it.

"I've got him," Sally announced, holding a green and brown stuffed animal.

"Sally!" Anna snapped. "I didn't give you permission to come in here!"

"I was just getting my stuffed turtle, Fred." Sally's voice

trembled. "This is Mom's room. It's where I usually stay, so I keep him under the bed."

"Well, you've got him now, so go to bed."

Sally clutched Fred tightly and scurried past Anna as she exited.

Alone at last, Anna changed into pajamas. She wrapped a matching robe around her waist and tied the sash. Then she picked up her cell phone, propped the pillows, and got comfortable. She scrolled through her newsfeed, emails, and Instagram to pass the time. When she was confident that Sally and Maura were asleep, she walked to the bathroom, wiped her face clean of makeup, and brushed her teeth.

Then she crept to the spare room across from hers and made a beeline for the closet. The door slid open quietly, revealing the box of DVDs between a container of yarn and a stack of *National Geographic* magazines. Anna placed the box on the mattress, then sat on the bed, her back to the hallway, and picked through the container. Using the flashlight on her phone, she found the DVD that the family had viewed earlier that evening and plucked it from its case. She rested the smooth iridescent disc on her fingers and placed her thumbs near the dime-sized opening in the center. It took more effort than she anticipated, but she soon heard the snap of the disk breaking in two.

The sound startled her. She froze and listened. The house was silent except for the sound of her own heart beating in her ears.

She reached into the box again and withdrew a case labeled "Family Vacation 2002." This time, she stepped into the closet and glided the door shut before snapping the disc in two. A rush of adrenaline surged through her body.

She slid the closet door open, grabbed the entire box of DVDs, and returned to the closet. She laid her phone on the floor so the flashlight would illuminate the tight space. Scanning the remaining contents, she happened upon a case titled "Old Home Movies." *Jackpot! This will hold Paul and Maura's wedding, the births of Dean and Stephanie, and so many more milestones.*

Anna was beside herself with glee as she snapped the disk in two and then snapped it again, sprinkling the shards into the box. For the next ten minutes, she repeated the process for every disc, each snap as intoxicating as the last.

When the box held nothing more than empty cases and shiny shards, she exited the closet. Then she tiptoed out of the room—only to encounter Sally coming out of the bathroom with Fred pinned beneath her arm.

"Aunt Anna! What were you doing in there?"

Anna drew a finger to her lips. "Shh, we don't want to wake Gran." Then she faked a giggle and spoke in a whisper. "I went downstairs for a snack and wandered into the wrong room." Smacking her forehead with her palm for effect, she added, "Silly me."

Sally covered her mouth and giggled, then took hold of Anna's hand and pulled her toward Stephanie's old room. "This is your room!"

"Thank you. Goodnight, Sally."

Anna closed the bedroom door and leaned against it, her back pressing into the wooden panels as she waited for her heart rate to slow. Then she turned down the bed and poured some water. *Thank goodness this will all be over tomorrow.*

* * * * * * * * * * * * * *

The sunrise painted the sky yellow and orange, the colors spilling in through the kitchen windows. Coffee cup in hand, Maura focused on her mental checklist as she prepared for her morning ride with Eric. It took her a moment to notice the treat awaiting her on the counter. A half dozen golden-brown muffins, walnuts peeking out from the tops, sat on a plate with a notecard perched like an army tent next to it.

> Maura,
> I baked you a breakfast treat. Thank you for your hospitality.
> From one chef to another,
> ~Anna

Maura smiled. *How thoughtful.* She peeled away the pastel-pink accordion paper encasing the muffin, and the smell of cinnamon and nutmeg invited her to take a bite.

Before she could sink her teeth into the moist spongy treat, her cell phone sounded. It was Stephanie. “Hi, Mom. Can you do me a big favor? I thought Kyle set his alarm, and he thought I set mine. Anyway, now I’m running late. Can you drive Sally to her game? It will really save me time if I can just meet you there.”

“No problem,” Maura said. “I’ll meet you in the parking lot.”

She left the muffin uneaten, popped her coffee cup in the dishwasher, and headed to the garage to prep her bike. At least she could get it ready now to save a little time later. After checking her air pressure, she opened the garage and attached her bike to the rack. She slid into the front seat, pressed the ignition button, and backed out of the garage, parking in the driveway.

* * * * * * * * * * * * *

Anna woke to the sound of Sally's voice.

"Hurry, Gran! I don't want to be late!"

"Coming. Just want to chill this water bottle for my bike ride; you won't be late." Maura placed the bottle in the fridge and grabbed the muffin.

Anna lay in bed, holding her breath until she heard the front door shut. Then she ran to the spare bedroom and peered out the window, watching as Maura backed onto the street.

What was with the bike on the back? Wasn't Stephanie supposed to pick up Sally?

Anna pulse quickened.

Why did I get up last night and put those muffins out? Idiot! You were too impatient!

She shook her head and recalled the only piece of advice her mother had ever given her: Nothing good ever comes from rushing.

Of course, that would be after her stepfather smacked Anna's knuckles with a yardstick because she hadn't cleaned the kitchen properly.

Anna dressed and inspected her tote. She took inventory of its contents and bounded down the stairs to the kitchen. As she suspected, one muffin was missing.

Not sure what to do next, she placed her bag on the floor and poured a cup of coffee.

* * * * * * * * * * * * *

Arriving home at 8:15, Maura figured she had more than enough time to run inside, change into her riding clothes, grab her bottle, and get to the park to meet Eric at nine. She removed her phone and ID from her purse and tossed them onto the passenger seat. She could slip them into the back pocket of her riding jersey later.

* * * * * * * * * * * * *

Anna's mind raced as she downed her coffee and paced. She jumped when she heard the front door open, followed by the padding of Maura's feet sprinting up the stairs.

* * * * * * * * * * * * *

Maura pulled on her riding shorts and slipped on a short-sleeve neon-green jersey. Paul had always insisted that she wear bright-colored clothing and attach blinking lights to the front and back of her bike for safety. It took a moment, but she realized that instead of a sinking feeling at the thought of Paul, she felt comfort at the thought of his concern for her safety. Then she glided her feet into flip-flops and bent down to grab her cycling shoes. The cleats made it possible to clip onto the pedals but impossible to walk gracefully.

Maura stood up and suddenly felt like she was on The Cyclone ride at the summer fair. She had sworn it off years ago due to its dizzying effects.

Maybe I stood up too quickly?

With just enough time left to grab her bottle and meet Eric, she brushed off the strange sensation and staggered down the stairs, clutching the railing to steady herself. But by the time she entered the kitchen, her tongue felt like it was coated in paste. A clammy sweat dotted her forehead. She swiped at it with a shaky hand.

"Maura, are you all right?" asked Anna. She pulled a chair away from the table, then took Maura by the arm and guided her to it.

Maura felt like the blood was draining from her body. Elbows on the table, she rested her head in her hands and closed her eyes.

Time became elusive. *Had only a moment passed—or had it been an hour?* Something tugged at her shins. She opened her eyes and scanned her surroundings, the mental fog lifting. She was in her kitchen. She'd felt oozy and Anna had helped her to a chair.

Before she could make sense of what had happened, Anna nimbly wrapped duct tape around her torso three times, pinning her arms to her side. Already, her legs were held fast to the chair.

Anna then took a seat across from Maura and wrapped her hands around her coffee mug. She studied Maura, savoring the older woman's confusion and helplessness. Maura's panic seemed tangible. Her pupils were dilated, her breath short and shallow.

"I understand you're confused," said Anna, "but this won't take long."

Maura had trouble formulating thoughts, much less words. She settled for staring at the young lady whom she'd welcomed so openly into her family.

"Do you have any idea about the kind of childhood I endured?" Anna said casually. She enjoyed her last swallow of coffee before continuing. "Of course you don't. Let me fill you in." She got up and refilled her coffee cup. "While you and your children were living here"—she made a sweeping gesture with her arm—"in the lap of luxury, I was living in a hovel in the middle of nowhere. My mother was a weak, defeated woman, and my stepfather abused everything. Alcohol, my mother… me."

Maura attempted to shift toward Anna, but the duct tape denied her. She looked into Anna's vacant eyes.

"The only thing that kept me going was the dream of getting away," Anna continued. "My mother didn't have the courage or strength to leave, but I promised myself at a young age that her fate would not be mine."

Maura noticed Anna's face soften.

"As a child," Anna said, "I used to lie in bed, dreaming that my real father would come to rescue my mother and me." She glared at Maura. "But he didn't."

As Maura closed her eyes in an attempt to focus on Anna's voice, a sting on her cheek startled her. *Had Anna just slapped her? What was happening? Why couldn't she talk?* As the sting faded, the subsequent throbbing hurt less than the insult of the action.

"Listen to me!" commanded Anna.

Maura forced her eyes to stay open, but the dizziness made it difficult to focus and listen at the same time.

"That's better. As I grew older, I began to hate my real father as much as my stepfather. How dare he abandon me? I made it my life's mission to become a success. My goal was to find him and make him explain how he could have rejected me. I was determined to show him the success he'd walked away from.

"As I got older, I understood how he was able to leave my mother. People grow apart. But I couldn't come to terms with him leaving *me*." The volume of her voice increased. "Not me—his own flesh and blood!"

Anna shook herself like a wet dog and composed herself. "You can imagine how thrilled I was when I found that letter hidden among my mother's belongings." She spoke more quickly as if the speed of her delivery might lessen the time she spent doubting Paul. "My father hadn't abandoned me, after all; he loved me and tried to take care of me." Her tone softened. "Now it all made sense. After finding that letter, I was certain that my mother tried to use the money to help me, but my stepfather wouldn't allow it. It wasn't until Dean and Stephanie reached out to me that it dawned on me." She leaned down and gripped the edges of Maura's chair, her forehead almost touching Maura's, and her voice rose to a shout. "You are as evil as my stepfather!"

Maura shook her head.

"Don't make me hit you again."

"I'm sorry, Anna, something is wrong with me."

"I laced your muffin with five hundred milligrams of weed."

Anna grabbed a muffin from the island and took a bite. "Not bad if I say so myself." She took another bite. "An adult dose is half a muffin, and you ate the entire thing!" She set the muffin down. "What kind of mother would go through life pretending her husband's child didn't—"

"Anna!" An electric jolt surged through Maura's body. "Sally ate a quarter of that muffin!"

"Sally, Sally, Sally! That brat almost blew my cover last night. Between barging into my room and prancing around the hall—"

"We have to let Stephanie know. I won't be able to live with myself if—"

"Funny you should say that." Anna opened her tote and pulled out a shiny six-inch chef's knife with a sleek black handle. She admired it as she rotated her wrist palm up, palm down, palm up, palm down. "This is the first knife I invested in after culinary school."

Maura struggled against the duct tape, but it wouldn't give. Sweat glistened on her upper lip as an adrenaline rush replaced the numbing effect of the weed. Her mind raced as she tried to formulate a plan, but she knew enough to feign confusion. She drew her eyebrows together and shook her head as if trying to clear her mind. "It's not too late to rethink this, Anna. Let me contact Stephanie, and I won't mention a word of this to anyone."

"Ha! Not only are you evil, but you're also pathetic."

"But you're a survivor. Look at all you've overcome." She spoke quickly, hoping Anna wouldn't stop her from talking. "Look at all you've accomplished. You're a renowned restaurant reviewer. Think of all the people who respect your opinion. You have every right to be bitter, but do you really want to throw that all away? You've become an icon in the culinary world."

Maura noticed that Anna seemed to be listening.

"Think back to when you were eight years old. I know how panicked I felt when the muffin started to take effect because I didn't know what was happening. But how must Sally feel? I know you understand firsthand what it's like to be a frightened and vulnerable child."

Maura fixed her stare on Anna. "From the bottom of my

heart, I am sorry. I'm sorry that you never got to know Paul. I'm sorry that I never pushed him to reach out to you. That was my insecurity, and you're right to resent me for that, but I know your DNA. It's the same DNA that made Stephanie and Dean search for you, once they learned you were their sister. It's the same DNA that made them want to meet you. It's the same DNA that made welcoming you into this family their only option."

Unsure if Anna's watery gaze was due to the marijuana taking effect or if she'd hit a nerve, Maura pleaded. "Anna, please, please let me contact your sister, Stephanie. Please let me help your niece, Sally, and I promise I won't ever mention this again."

Anna's clenched fist, which had been tapping the knife on the tabletop, came to a rest.

"I've been dreaming about this moment since Dean invited me to his house. I mean, really? Celebrating Father's Day with all of you? It was like rubbing salt in the wound. You created this life with my father, slammed the door shut, locked it, and threw away the key."

Anna wandered to the kitchen sink and scanned the patio. A fiberglass table and chairs invited family feasts; a seating area, with tropical print cushions, beckoned jovial conversations. She spun around and returned to her seat at the farm table.

"When I arrived that day, I had a plan. If you remember, I had a rental car. I planned to feign exhaustion and ask if I could spend the night at your house. Then I was going to ask if we could have tea and bring out the muffins that I'd conveniently forgotten to share at Dean's." She nodded toward the muffins. "I mean, really, who could resist one?" She grinned, then continued. "I had my duct tape and trusty knife, and I knew it wouldn't be hard to get you into the exact predicament you find yourself in right now."

Anna sighed and shrugged her shoulders. "Two things happened that day at Dean's house that made me rethink my plan. First, it dawned on me that someone might notice a car with New York license plates at your house. I knew it wouldn't take long for the car to be traced back to me. And second, you invited me here for July Fourth." She extended her arms, her upturned palms punctuating her emotion. "I hit the jackpot. Everyone knew that I was taking the eleven-fifteen train, and I knew that after your ride, I could take care of business here and have more than enough time to run to the station and head back to Manhattan."

Maura couldn't believe what she was hearing, but she forced herself to remain stoic, knowing that reacting might set Anna off.

"As has been pointed out," Anna continued, "athleticism is in my DNA. When we were watching those old home movies, I could have vomited, hearing about what a great baseball player Paul had been and how he coached Dean's team. And then the accolades poured over Dean like syrup on a pancake. 'Oh, Anna, Dean held the record for stolen bases that year. He ran so fast.'" She glared at Maura. "I was a fast runner too. Running became the only way for me to escape my stepfather and my life. I even went to college on a track scholarship. And thank God for that because as far as I knew, there was no money for college."

In an attempt to appeal to the vulnerable child hidden deep within Anna's psyche, Maura spoke up. "That's exactly what I was referring to earlier. I see so many similarities between you, Paul, Dean, and Stephanie. Not only are you athletic, tenacious, and goal-driven, but you have many of the same mannerisms as your father. Dean and Stephanie noticed them as soon as they met you."

Maura detected a look of curiosity on Anna's face.

"Right now, the way you're leaning forward, focusing on my every word—Paul did the same exact thing."

Anna cleared her throat. "Really?"

Maura opened her eyes wide. "There! Your father used to clear his throat like that when he was unsure of something." Anna's shoulders dropped, perhaps a sign that she was becoming more intrigued and relaxed. "And your easy manner—you fit right in with everyone as soon as you met them. Not everyone can do that, but your father and sister can. Of course, your attention to detail, which makes you a successful restaurant critic, is so much like Dean, it's eerie. I meant what I said: you are undeniably a part of this family. Please, Anna, don't lose this chance at being a sister and an aunt. Everyone is thrilled at the prospect of a future that includes you. It's about time you claim your place in the family's legacy."

Maura watched as Anna stared into space for what felt like an eternity. Precious moments were slipping away, and Maura had to get to Sally.

"I dreamt of being part of a family just like this for my entire life," said Anna, "and I almost threw it away." She inhaled deeply. Her exhalation was pronounced, as if she were expelling all the toxins she'd harbored for so long. "You're right, Maura. I was so bitter that I couldn't see my chance at being part of a family—this family. It's a dream come true, and I almost threw it all away." Trying to stave off the wave of emotion about to swallow her, she cleared her throat once more. Knife in hand, she approached Maura. “I’ll cut the duct tape and you—”

A porch chair crashed through the back door. Eric flew through the hole, darting across the room and tackling Anna.

“Maura!” he shouted. “Are you all right?”

“Sally!” she screamed.

“What about Sally?”

“Get off of me!” shrieked Anna.

The loud bang of a door being kicked open resonated from the foyer.

“We’re here! In the kitchen!” yelled Eric as he pressed his knees into Anna’s arms. Two police officers with weapons drawn ran into the kitchen.

CHAPTER 30

"You can't stop the waves, but you can learn to surf."

— Joseph Goldstein

The brightly colored metallic chairs—possibly an attempt at whimsical design—did little to lighten the mood in the community hospital waiting room.

"Mom!" cried Stephanie as she jumped up to greet Maura and Eric. She wrapped her arms around Maura and sobbed into her neck, her tears dampening Maura's shoulder.

"How is Sally?" asked Maura.

Stephanie inched back, wiping her eyes with the back of her wrist as Kyle stepped forward and handed her a tissue. "We're still waiting to meet with the doc," Kyle said. "She's running some tests." Kyle turned to Eric and extended his hand. "I'm Stephanie's husband, Kyle."

"I'm Eric. So sorry to meet you under these circumstances.

Why don't you all sit down, and I'll get us some coffee?"

Stephanie and Kyle listened intently as Maura recounted the events of the morning. Other than when her voice quivered as she described sharing the muffin with Sally in the car, her delivery was as methodical as if she were an observer of the event rather than the victim.

She finished just as Eric returned.

"I know I said it over the phone, but I'm so glad you're all right," blubbered Stephanie. "First losing Dad, and then Anna trying to… Sally's got to be okay!"

"Stephanie, listen to me," said Maura. "We will get through this. Whatever the future holds, we will get through it. Trust me."

Kyle turned to Eric. "How did you know to look for Maura?"

"As you know, your Mom's training for a triathlon, and I'm training with her. We were supposed to meet this morning for a ride and run, and when she didn't show up, I was concerned, but I assumed she had just overslept. It wasn't until she didn't answer any texts or calls that I got worried." Eric leaned back, pressing his spine against the cold metal back of the chair. "I decided to ride toward her house in the hope of meeting her on the way." He rubbed his hands up and down his thighs.

"When I got to the house, I was surprised to see her car parked in the driveway with her bike attached to the rack, and even more startled when I peered into the driver's window and saw her cell phone lying on the front seat." Eric shifted in his chair. "I knew something wasn't right, so I ran to the front porch and tried to enter the house. I didn't even pause to ring the bell. The door was locked, so I checked the backyard. Nothing. So I headed to the screened porch, thinking maybe the back door was open. Then I glanced through the window and saw your mother duct-taped to the chair with Anna across from her."

"Oh my gosh," exclaimed Stephanie.

"I ran back to the side of the house and called 911."

Maura, sitting beside Eric, gasped as she reached over and squeezed his forearm. "That's why Anna didn't see you when she went to the kitchen window and looked outside."

"The dispatcher told me that they had a squad car in the vicinity," explained Eric. "He told me not to do anything but watch until they got there." Eric took a deep breath. "I crept back to the window and peered inside. It was clear that an intense conversation was going on. Then all of a sudden, Anna sprang up, knife in hand, and made her move!"

Eric jumped up, grabbed the empty chair to his right, and hoisted it toward the ceiling. "I snagged a chair and smashed it through—"

"Sir!" shouted a security guard, dashing over with his hand on his holster.

"It's cool, I'm sorry!" Eric said. "I was telling a story and got carried away."

"Mr. and Mrs. O'Brien," called a young woman in pink scrubs. "The doctor is ready to meet with you."

"Mom, come with us," pleaded Stephanie.

"I'll wait here," said Eric.

They followed the young woman, who led them to an elevator and directed them to go to the fourth floor, room 4110. As they ascended, Maura stared at the red digitized floor numbers on the panel. *Dear God, please let Sally be all right.* The doors slid open, and Stephanie sprinted down the hall.

A few seconds later, Kyle and Maura rushed in behind her.

The aqua walls, swimming with sea life, did little to mask the antiseptic overtones of the space. Sally was asleep, an IV attached to her forearm, and an oxygen tube in her nose.

"Mr. and Mrs. O'Brien," said a small dark-haired woman with a slight Spanish accent.

"Please tell us she'll be all right," begged Stephanie.

"It was very helpful to know that she ingested that muffin. Often, when children present with the symptoms that Sally did—difficulty walking, extreme sleepiness, respiratory distress, and the like—we spend a good deal of time administering tests to search for the cause. Luckily for Sally, this wasn't the case. We've checked her urine, and she is still showing a small amount of THC, the main psychoactive ingredient in marijuana. However, she doesn't seem to be experiencing hallucinations, and her breathing is no longer labored. Most importantly, the MRI showed no signs of brain damage."

Maura, Kyle, and Stephanie released a collective sigh.

"We'd still like to keep her overnight for observation. Mom and Dad, you are welcome to stay with her for the remainder of her stay. But I feel strongly that by tomorrow, she will be just fine."

"Thank you," said Kyle as Stephanie threw her arms around Maura, who until that moment had been standing next to Sally and stroking her hair.

"If you don't have any questions, I'll see you in the morning," said Dr. Sanchez as she exited.

"I'm going to leave you three alone," Maura said. "You two just focus on this little angel."

Maura returned to the waiting room to find Eric staring at the screen of his cell phone. She sat down next to him and waited a few moments until he realized she had returned.

"Maura!" His flushed neck revealed his surprise. "How long have you been sitting there? I was just dealing with a situation at the travel agency and—"

Tears cascaded down Maura's cheeks. Unable to speak, she shook her head. Eric slipped an arm around her shoulders and pulled her close. "It's okay, Maura. It'll be okay." He tightened his grasp. "I'm so sorry."

Maura sat up straight and patted her cheeks with her fingertips, then wiped them dry on the front of her shirt.

Eric reached into the back pocket of his jersey. "Here, take this," he said as he handed her a bandana.

She accepted his offering and grinned warmly. "I'm sorry, Sally's fine!"

Eric wrinkled his forehead.

"The doctor said that she wants to keep her overnight for observation, but she should be fine by tomorrow morning."

"Wow, that's great," said Eric, the puzzled look still evident. "It's just that when you started to cry, I assumed..."

Maura folded her arms, hugging them close to her chest. "I don't know what happened; I saw you and was just overcome with emotion."

"You've been through the wringer today. Come on, let's get out of here."

* * * * * * * * * * * * *

Maura peeled off her riding shorts and jersey and stepped into the steamy shower enclosure. She closed her eyes and lost herself in the sensation of water pelting her head and shoulders. Scrubbing every square inch of her body with a soapy washcloth, she attempted to wash away the atrocities of the day. Her upper arms and shins were tender—reminders of the duct tape that had bound her to the chair.

Out of the shower, she dried off, slipped into a T-shirt and shorts, and ran a comb through her wet hair before heading downstairs. The plywood nailed to the front door by Dean was yet another reminder of the horror of the day.

"Perfect timing," said Eric as Maura entered the kitchen. He pulled out a stool at the island and gestured for her to sit, then he removed the cork from a bottle of Sauvignon Blanc and filled the wine glass resting at the edge of the flowered placemat. Turning to the stove, he spooned a mound of fluffy eggs onto a plate and wedged a piece of toast next to the soft yellow scramble.

"For you, madam," he said in an attempt at a French accent. "Breakfast for dinner. Bon appétit!" He placed his free hand on the small of his back and bowed before setting down the plate. "I hope you don't mind me making myself at home in your kitchen, but it occurred to me that you hadn't eaten anything all day. Well, except for that muffin."

"Don't remind me!"

Eric shrugged. "I'm not much of a cook, but I do make a mean scrambled egg."

"Thank you, but what about you?"

"I had a quick bite when you were checking on Sally. Besides, this isn't about me. It's about you, and that said, I am going to leave you to enjoy this scrumptious meal and relax. Something tells me that after you eat, exhaustion is going to hit you like a ton of bricks. I'll check in with you tomorrow."

"But—"

"No buts, young lady." He stepped forward and brushed

back a wave of hair from her face.

Maura's heartbeat quickened.

"Eat and get some rest. I'll talk to you tomorrow."

EPILOGUE

"It's not about time, it's about choices.

How are you spending your choices?"

— *Beverly Adamo*

Beep-beep-beep… Maura's alarm jolted her out of a much-needed, deep sleep. The morning sun shone through the blinds, the slats casting a shadow of muted stripes on the cream-colored blanket. She propped her pillow against the cherry wood headboard of the old four-poster bed, sat up, and looked around the room. The last several days had been as emotional as they'd been exhausting.

A stack of boxes was piled high in the corner, one labeled winter clothes, another labeled shoes, and a third labeled bedding. It had been two years, and Maura knew it was time to move on, not only from this house—a place that held memories both treasured and devastating—but onto the next chapter of her life. She ran through the day's checklist. After a steaming mug of coffee, she would prepare for the afternoon's "moving-on celebration."

* * * * * * * * * * * * *

"I've got the drinks and ice," announced Eric as he nudged the front door shut with his hip. He made his way down the hall to find Maura at the kitchen sink. Wrapping his arms around her from behind, he gave her a squeeze before spinning her around to face him.

"How are you doing?" he asked.

Maura leaned forward and pressed her lips to his, letting them linger there before she leaned back. "I'm good."

Eric bent forward for one more peck. "I don't want it to get too hot in here or this ice might melt." He winked, picked up the bag of ice, and headed for the cooler out back.

For the next hour, they worked in tandem preparing for their guests. At two o'clock, Sally ran into the kitchen holding a package the size of a magazine wrapped in bright green paper with a pink bow.

"I can't wait for you to open your 'house-cooling' gift!"

"What's a house-cooling gift?" Maura asked.

"Mom told me that when someone moves into a new house, they get a housewarming gift. But since you're moving out of this house, this must be a house-cooling gift. But you have to wait until later to open it."

Stephanie came in and placed a large bowl on the island before giving Maura a hug.

"Hi, honey, where are Kyle and Jake?"

"They're out back giving Eric a hand."

"Hey, Mom," called Dean as he entered from the front hall.

He bent down and wrapped his arms tightly around Maura, lifting her off the ground.

"Dean! Put me down," she squealed.

"Hi, everyone, I'm going out back," called Sam as he ran through the kitchen. "Come on, Sally, I have water balloons."

"Sam brings the fun," said Maddie. "Tell me what I can do to help." She moved toward Maura, giving her a quick hug.

Before Maura could answer, another voice called from the foyer. "Woo-hoo!"

"We're in the kitchen. Come and join us."

"I just want to warn you, you may want to put on some sunglasses," said Nicole as she and Harris entered the kitchen. She extended her hand to highlight the sparkling diamond on her left ring finger.

"Oh my gosh," exclaimed Maura. "Congratulations!"

"Who are we congratulating and why?" asked Lonnie as she entered the kitchen from the back door.

"Harris and I," said Nicole as she turned her extended hand toward Lonnie. "Hold on, why is your shoulder wet?"

"I got hit by a stray water balloon in the backyard. No worries, I won't melt." She ran to Nicole and embraced her. "Congratulations!" She released Nicole and hugged Harris.

"Does this mean what I think it does?" said Kara as she dropped a bag of dinner rolls onto the table and bolted to Nicole.

"What did I miss?" asked Josie as she entered the kitchen, a bottle of champagne in each hand. "Do we have even more to celebrate?"

"Harris proposed!" said Nicole as she extended her left arm once more, showing off the shiny bauble on her finger.

"I'm so happy for you both," said Josie as she set the

champagne bottles on the table and moved toward the happy couple.

* * * * * * * * * * * * * * *

Later, with everyone gathered in the kitchen, Dean presented Maura with the family gift. "We thought this would be a fitting token for you to bring along in the next phase of your life," said Dean.

She peeled back the paper to reveal a framed watercolor of the house.

Clutching it to her chest, Maura sighed. "This is perfect. Thank you all so much. I know the past two years haven't been easy for any of us, but please know how thankful I am to have gone through it with all of you by my side." She smiled at Dean and Stephanie. "Leaving this house is bittersweet; we have so many memories here." She glanced at Josie. "But the transition is easier knowing that while I'm house-sitting for Josie the next two years, I can decide where and with whom"—she smiled at Eric—"I want to settle. And it's certainly comforting to know that Kara and Jack will be my neighbors."

Maura raised her glass. "Josie, I know I speak for everyone here when I say that Thailand's gain is our loss. We are so proud of you for seeing a cherished goal to fruition. The Peace Corps is lucky to have you." After a sip of champagne, she continued. "Speaking of goals, I conducted my last cooking class a few nights ago."

"You enjoyed teaching those classes so much," said Stephanie. "It's a shame it has to come to an end. I know it's not feasible if you're not in this kitchen, but—"

"As the saying goes, when one door closes, another one opens. Lonnie and I have decided to collaborate on a book. We're calling it, *It's a Marathon, Not a Sprint,* and it will chronicle her journey to healthy eating, supplemented with my recipes. And did I mention that it will also include her journal entries as I help her train for her first half-marathon?"

Everyone burst into boisterous applause.

Maura stood and looked at her grandchildren perched on stools at the island, where so many meals had been prepared and served. She scanned the faces of her family and friends, then raised her glass one last time. "Here's to the future. Whatever it may bring, we'll see it through together. To us!"

"To us!" the group echoed.

When everyone had gone, and the house was quiet, Maura sat down at the table alone and penned a letter.

Dear Anna,

I don't expect a response to this note, but I wanted to let you know that I'm moving out of the family home and on with my life.

Since the last time I saw you, I've had a lot of time to reflect. I've taken ownership of the choices I made and have come to understand that those choices—both good and bad—resulted in consequences, the effects of which resonate to this day. I've also realized that I was doing the best

> I could with the information I had at the time, and I've forgiven myself. I hope you can forgive me as well. I should have insisted that Paul be present for you, but I was selfish and didn't want to share him.
>
> I'm sorry things worked out the way they did. You deserved better. I can't justify what you attempted to do, but I do forgive you.
>
> Anna, you are in my thoughts daily.
>
> Be well,
> Maura
>
> P.S. Over time I've learned that it's not about getting second chances, it's about taking them. I hope you'll take all of yours.

Maura pushed the letter aside and reached for the box she'd brought down from the spare bedroom, where Anna had gleefully cracked the family DVDs. That room now housed a contraption that allowed Maura to spin indoors on her road bike all winter while she participated in virtual bike races. And the closet contained the wetsuit Maura had worn during the Half Ironman she'd completed in Rio with Eric. Tomorrow she would pack it all up along with the race medals she'd earned over the past two years. But now it was time to move on.

She rummaged through the box. A stack of newspaper clippings was tucked under the scrap of paper she'd been searching for. She pulled it out and copied the address and inmate number onto the envelope:

> Anna Anderson #255483
> Edna Martin Correctional Facility for Women
> Martinsdale, NJ 08773

****** THE END ******

Acknowledgments

Tim Morrison and Mike Lubniewski, thank you for guiding me through the early stages of my manuscript. Thank you, Anne McAneny, for your invaluable editorial work. I want you all to know that your suggestions and guidance made a potentially daunting passion project a true pleasure.

Thanks also to my future daughter-in-law, Juliana Gyimesi, for capturing the essence of the story with your exquisite cover design.

I can't thank Christine Waltsak enough for helping me design a website and manage social media in anticipation of many satisfied Supper Clubbers.

In addition, thank you to my mother, Jane, my mother-in-law, Rosanne, and my sister-in-law, Karen, all of whom read early drafts. Thank you to my children—Timothy, Molly, and Seamus—who make me want to be my best. And thank you to friends, including but not limited to Ginny, Betty, Elaine, Jane, Laurie, Sandi, Kathleen, Jen, and Heather—and everyone at "the farm"—all of whom seemed to magically appear with encouragement and connections just when I needed them.

I can't leave out the women of the TAC locker room, who were the impetus for the story. There's a little piece of each of you embedded in the pages.

And finally, I'm so grateful to my husband, Peter, who always makes me believe I can do anything. Thanks to you, I've checked off one more item on my bucket list!

About the Author

Susan Higgins-Krais lives at the Jersey Shore, where she taught school for over thirty years while raising a family. After retiring, she worked in the fitness industry but has now dedicated herself full-time to writing. *It's About Time*, her debut novel, is Book One of the Supper Club Chronicles.

Susan is hard at work on Book Two of the Supper Club Chronicles, slated for release in early 2021. To hear about the book's progress and receive an opportunity to name a character, sign up for Susan's email list here. You'll receive occasional Supper Club updates and recipes, and you can enter for a chance to win Susan's attendance at your virtual supper club meeting! Your email address will never be shared, and you can opt out at any time.

Susan loves to hear from readers. Connect with her in any of the following ways:

Website: SusanHigginsKrais.com
Facebook: Susan Higgins-Krais/Author
Instagram: susan_higginskrais@Instagram
Email: susanhigginskrais@gmail.com

Special Request directly from Susan: If you enjoyed this book, please consider leaving a review on the site of your choice. Reviews are difficult to come by but very much appreciated by authors like me. Thank you, and bon appétit!

Book Club Discussion Questions

1. DNA test results play a central role in the story. Have you ever taken a DNA test? Why or why not?
2. Maura and Paul's marriage was impacted by secrets. How did you feel when Maura's secret was revealed? How did you react when Paul's secret was discovered? Do you think there is ever a time when keeping a secret from your partner is acceptable?
3. Maura invites her locker room friends to join her for dinner and "The Supper Club" is created. How important is it for people to belong to a tribe?
4. In addition to exercise and cooking, Maura relies on a therapist to help navigate her new normal. How do you feel about therapy? Are you a proponent of traditional therapy or have you found another way to work through problems and issues?
5. Staying married to Paul was a decision Maura made for the good of the children. What are your feelings about divorce when children are involved?
6. Maura and Josie discuss love after loss. Whose view do you most relate to, Maura's or Josie's, and why?
7. The friends discuss ageism. Do you believe age to be a factor in the workplace and in society in general, or is the idea a vehicle for older people to deflect diminishing skills and abilities?

8. Kara moves to the same adult community that Josie lives in, and Maura eventually ends up there as well. What is your opinion of fifty-five-and-older communities? Discuss the pros and cons of living in that setting.

9. At the end of the story, Maura convinces Anna to reconsider and embrace the family she always dreamed of. Do you think Maura was sincere? Did she say those things from the heart or was it just a ploy?

10. In the epilogue, Maura makes a plea to Anna to embrace second chances. Given the circumstances of both of their lives, how much were they each impacted by fate versus free will?

Made in the USA
Middletown, DE
01 September 2020

17239633R00154